References

The quotes from M. Maier Atalanta Fugiens, Oppenheim 1618 (Chap. IV) and The Opus Magnum (Chap. VII) are contained in "Alchemy & Mysticism" by Alexander Roob (Taschen, 1997).

The references to the work of painter Pat Moran (in chapter XIII) are inspired by my acquaintance with the painter and his work as well as a posthumously prepared exhibition and catalogue "Pat Moran (1961 - 1992) A Retrospective" (Gandon Editions, 2003).

Thanks to

John O'Dea and Sligo's Solo Festival; Vivienne Lavery; Jim King, Donal O'Kelly, Joe O'Byrne and Colm Hackett.

Editor: Adam Hyland
Lay-out and Cover Design: Daragh Stewart

First Published: 2009
Publisher: Bandit Films, Dromahair, Co. Leitrim www.banditfilms.ie
Printed by: Turner Print Group, Longford
printed on recycled paper
A copy of this book has been lodged with the National Library of Ireland
ISBN: 978-0-9563052-0-6

Contents

Prologue

I was the he of it, the she of it, the it of them all as they became one. It's down to me to tell their stories, not least because their stories are now my story.

After the years of enforced absence from these streets I began to miss them. On re-acquaintance with my unholy Trinity, I realised what I disliked most was how dishonest each was with the other to the point of betrayal. That's poets for you; unable to differentiate between fact and fiction: always prepared to twist the truth.

Yes, we could have been kinder to one another. We invaded each others' lives, even as we slept, borrowed and stole from each other. We were rarely where we said we were for fear of predictability, or discovery.

In the end, I stole from them more than they from me; identities, thoughts, dreams. Believe me, if one or another of them had prevailed in the joust that was to unfold, I wouldn't be telling this story. They underestimated me. I was never there to be a mere muse.

A poet consumes all around them before turning this stuff into words. Above all, poets consume each other. That's how they learn and grow. Yes, I hijacked their voices as well as their mistakes, so that I could make them my own, so that I could reinvent myself. Where's the crime? I stole from them and stole from myself until I was unable to distinguish whose was what. So, I admit it. I am an unreconstructed thief.

I loved them all, Jack, Skiddy, Rosa too. One muse to the sacred and the profane, in which order must await the telling of their tale. My unholy Trinity. If I were to meet them, I might not even recognise them or differentiate. In your real world they don't exist anymore, certainly not as they did. The city where they discovered themselves and each other no longer exists. Only in fragments and those fragments are memories. But why feel nostalgic for a time that nobody but I appears to mourn? After all, the city that nurtured them with tough love has consumed itself to become other than it was.

So have I.

I
Self-less City, 1988

They lived in a city of ghosts. Not her ghosts. His ghosts. The ghosts of his family, their forbearers, the ghosts of all the once living now dead martyrs and myriad poets. The immortal words and deeds of these dead poets clung to the city like a sarcophagus within which the city was gradually decaying. It had become a city without a self, merely a long and baleful memory that was an excuse for a self.

Walls crumbled, well aided by reckless application of the wrecking ball. Drugs flowed into the arms of the dispossessed. Leaders were incapable of kicking their addictions to backhanders. Youth and promise had fled to greener pastures. The country of which this city stood as uncertain capital and from which it drew its power was slowly bleeding from a dirty 30-year war to the north. Finally, the reins of power were now in the grip of a man who had grown rich plundering the city's earlier promise through abuse of high office, bribery and corruption, despite a professed dedication to poets and poetry.

Perhaps it was out of a sleepy realisation of this decline that the City Fathers had declared this unpromising year of 1988 as the celebration year for the city's Millennium. Their Millennium had little basis in fact, something to do with the arrival of the Vikings into the black pool, as if the black pool had not existed prior to that date. Given that the same City Fathers had done their best a decade before to destroy what remained of that historic Viking settlement by the black pool their millennial declaration was correctly seen as a bad joke. By the third damp wintry month of the year there was little sign of the celebrations getting off the ground and this depression year of 1988 was proving to be little different than the last. At best it would turn out to be a celebration of the dreams of futures past.

The rattle of the mud-guard against the back-wheel of his bike intensified as Jack Lennon glided towards the lights at the head of Westmoreland Street. Pedestrians had already pushed up for a rush hour charge across the bridge; buses and trains to catch out of the city's cool and smoggy air. A winter the quixotic chaotic exotic neurotic urban word warrior and burgeoning bicycle poet had been wishing away from the door of his drab native city. He lacked a self and believed this to be a positive thing. It left him open to the world. For him, the city like the personality was a hollow space within the sarcophagus of history to be filled by actions, determined by Events.

Yes, city and country were threatening to implode, but this imminent collapse would result, he believed, in the creation of something better, something bigger. Perhaps his headlong rush to the future was motivated by the recent experience of his own life, an attempt to resist gravity and above all the suck of the gaping grave into which he had recently gazed. Perhaps he was just made this way. For now, he lived in a state of empathy with the city: lean, impoverished, quietly melancholic for that loss he could not yet describe or even acknowledge.

The waves of commuters remained parted long enough for Jack to seize the initiative. Nature abhors a vacuum. He was ready to fill this one when he realised that the hordes were not holding off to his command but to that of the Number Ten Bus accelerating angrily on his shoulder. With a burst of pedal power he beat the red light and now set his bespectacled sights on the lights on the far side of the bridge. With all the muster of his taut frame and availing of the slight incline the bridge allowed for the traveller northwards (the north quay being imperceptibly lower than the south denoting its status in this divided city of have and have not) he resolved to beat the bus to the next stop.

The driver drew his bus alongside with the slyest of glances, playing him like a cat with a mouse. Too many encounters with the crusty bus-drivers of these oily streets had given Jack a veteran edge at the tender age of 24. His quest now seemed hopeless and he was about to cede victory when a wayward pedestrian, a legal clerk at the Four Courts rushing home to make dinner for his invalided mother perhaps, was preparing to step into his path. Judging the poet-cyclist of a lower order he stepped off the kerb. Jack deftly responded by mounting the kerb, forcing the clerk further into the traffic. The frustrated bus-driver applied the breaks. The clerk visibly whitened at the prospect of pre-deceasing his mother, as the bus breezed his shook face, Jack his arse. A burst of acceleration and Jack was past him and back on the street. He rode the amber to angry horns, leaving the stalling bus in his wake.

The majesty of O'Connell Street opened itself to him. At full sail now he pulled into the centre lane and took his hands casually off the bars to absorb the buzz, the sellers of Herald or Press, Herald or Press.

Herald or Press won't ease your distress. Chimes from the Lir clock lamented the passing of the rare auld times, adding further to the cacophony of past and future. Herald or Press. Herald or Press. A woman in the crowd drew his eye, dragging her kids and bags of shopping through the rush hour melée. Jack recognised her from his travels through the city and surveyed as she stopped and turned to hurry her children on, making a clearing in the pedestrian tide outside Easons while scattering some peddlers of obscure religious sects as she ushered her children back under her wing. A determined gesture even these soul-hunters of the depression years - Mormons, Moonies, Hari Krishnas - must obey. You won't catch me, Jack Lennon, 100 per cent Marxist rationalist empiricist, with your mumbo jumbo.

The wobble of the package on his back carrier distracted him from a polemical discourse with Moonies and Co and he lowered his hands to take hold of the steering as he passed the back gates to Brian "Beanstalk" Brennan's Prince's Publishing Demesne. From mere beans are such empires made. Herald or Press. Herald or Press. Media is big business. Past the GPO with a silent nod to the Poet Revolutionaries: Pearse dead in a hail of bullets at an age not much greater than Jack's.

Nothing as glorious as blood sacrifice promised from the poetry wars in which Jack Lennon was currently engaged, but things were beginning to get a bit strange. Why was Terry Crowe, his ex-literacy student in Mountjoy sending him cassettes? It was only a month since Tony had told him he never wanted to see his specky face again. The cassette had been slipped to him as he hurried into the printers earlier that day by a young fellow on a bike who had merely said "this is for you". As ink dried on the print run Jack had listened to the meandering reflections from Terry on life in Gaol, his family and the north-side Hardwicke Street community from which his incarceration had separated him. Was Terry venting his anger at Jack, however misplaced, by sending him the tape? Did he want to resume his literacy class?

Jack had more pressing problems to deal with, which had to do with people at liberty. If he just kept moving maybe these problems would fall away. A lone horse travels faster, he heard a voice say. What about Rosa? How could she fit in to that plan? Did he fit into hers? He seemed to be proving a burden to her of late as the crises mounted. The day at the printers had taken his mind off the financial crisis which was about to form the subject of the meeting to which he was hurrying two minutes off the pace. Debts might catch up, but he must outstrip time, resist the suck of the grave. Something told him that a solution to the indebtedness of the Dublin Poetry Collective, for which he was being held personally responsible by their previous printer, required more than just another meeting.

The regular ruck of tea-time travellers loitered around the Number Ten bus stop as Jack manoeuvred his bike off the well-oiled surface of Parnell Square. As he moved he felt the crowd move too, not to oblige him but to establish position for the already heaving bus approaching. Their shuffle revealed to Jack a lone figure lying hunched in a snail-like position on the street. It was the same man who had lain on the street since morning, crouched and hooded. His prostrate form appeared as if bowing towards mecca, only mecca was some 90 degrees in a clockwise direction. Jack calculated he had progressed a mere ten paces in as many hours. He must be freezing. Was he planning to pass the coming night in this painstaking position. Jack checked his watch and scanned the emptying square. Resting his bike against the flaking ironwork that encircled the door-step he noticed that other bikes had been tethered to the railings despite his entreaties to his fellow collective members to conceal them in the ample foyer of this Georgian edifice.

On approach, the figure appeared more as one of those yogic penatents Rosa had shown him in her book on Indian meditation. He thought it best not to interrupt the meditation. However, he noticed that a film of rain was beginning to stain the khaki jacket of the mysteriously hooded figure. He was curious too and felt the man was now aware of his presence by his side. Jack laid a hand on his shoulder. He noticed how muscled and warm it felt despite the hours in the open. He ventured a meek and unthreatening "hello?". His actions appeared to evince little reaction and he was about to retreat when the body emitted a jerking motion as if stirred from deep sleep. The head turned slowly as if surfacing from some dream state. Jack was backing off when the head quickly jerked in his direction. He stood transfixed as glassy searching eyes were laid upon him. The lips moved as if beckoning some far off and unformed words. Jack strained to hear.
- Don't you know who I am?
Jack shook his head in bewildered fashion. Should he know?
- Who are you?
- I...I am a scaffolder!

The voice was so phlegm-laden that the words barely escaped his lips. Jack dispelled the yogic interpretation and realised from his appearance that this scaffolder had come from a building site, as evidenced by the cement dust on his clothes, and was now merely a little the worse for wear. What chilled him was the intensity with which the man said these few simple words. "I am a scaffolder". It felt personal, as if he knew Jack. All Jack could do was shake his head. Realising the man had no intention of standing up and fearing a confrontation Jack uttered a plaintive "sorry" and retreated to the entrance of number 105 where he hurriedly unlocked the door and wheeled his bike into the damp and darkened hallway.

Half way up the broad crooked stairs of this yawning building that had formerly served as the Hi Brasil Hotel, his thin fingers were tingling with lack of oxygen as he remembered he hadn't eaten since breakfast, big black bits skating across his vision like the floating islands of Lake Titicaca. The face of the scaffolder, those searching eyes, remained imprinted on his vision while his own heavy breathing reverberated on the landing that led to the poets' haven, past the fading posters of cultural and solidarity events: Poets For Nicaragua, Poets Against Repression, Poets Against The Bomb, Poet boot against the door. Five Fifty Nine.

Jack's dramatic entrance to the office of the Dublin Poetry Collective went unnoticed. Expecting to lift the downbeat atmosphere of his fellow poets for whom he was bringing home the bacon, he found an air of frenzied industry as said poets, led by Rosa, buzzed around like worker bees or happy coffee pickers in a Nicaraguan plantation. Light-headed Jack looked for a place to rest the box of poetry bulletins. He'd have arms as long as Dan Donnelly, the famous Kildare pugilist, if he didn't relieve himself of this box of poetry. The business-like Rosa approached, duster in hand, and waved it at the lower shelf where all the back issues of the bulletin dwelled. This was no back issue. A defiant Jack planted the box on the central table that had just been cleared for their meeting and retreated towards the window to survey the street. The scaffolder remained in position, despite the pumping clouds now drenching the street and the Garden of Remembrance beyond. He should go back down and insist he come into the shelter of the hallway. After all this building was once a hotel. In many ways it still was.

He turned in distraction as Rosa swiped the box of poetry bulletins off

the table and replaced it with a colourful throw.
- He'll be here any minute.
She addressed his rare moment of idleness. Jack mused on the kind of visitor whose arrival could penetrate their hermetically sealed existence and so easily supersede the arrival of The Monthly Poetry Bulletin. Rosa caught his eye and brightened.
- He has an announcement.
If it wasn't the printer who owned their bad debts, could it be the dole arriving with an offer of amnesty for all poets earning a few bob on the side from flogging their wares; that woman from Jobquest who had landed him and a couple of the others with the literacy scheme up at the prison now offering to put them on a start-your-own-business scheme? Or the landlord finally wise to Jack's use of his building? His landlord, the owner of multiple Georgian buildings throughout the city, knew Jack as an aspirant poet, but nothing of the brace of poets for whom he was running a glorified day shelter.
- Can't you do something useful?
Rosa stared at him ashen-faced. Jack was aware his stock was low with his fellow poets given the failure of recent money-making initiatives, but why was Rosa losing patience with him too? After all, he was making amends. He was up to his neck in amends.
- Who?
- Who what?
Rosa was now winding up the hoover.
- Rosa, I don't know who or what ...
They were already sounding like an old husband and wife. Arlene, the Poetry Collective's book-keeper of sorts, already up to high-do, cowered in the corner. Rosa had been working her to the bone and she looked dizzy, even more confounded than Jack by the rate of activity.

Jack was distracted by the rattle of delft and the sound of hollow footsteps descending from the top floor heralding the arrival into the room of fellow poet S.K.Dee, a tray of cups and assorted biscuits from Rosa and Jack's kitchen under his charge. Skiddy, as he was known to his fellow poets for his poor hygiene and reptilian ways, making tea for others? Must be something in it for him.
- Who?
He demanded in a far too plaintive voice.
- Jenkins, gobshite!
Skiddy's retort pushed Jack further to the edge of events.

Skiddy employed this earthy rural patois with Jack to make it seem like

he was more man of the people, though Jack knew that the tree-lined avenues around Taylor's Hill in Galway City where Skiddy had been brought up were far from muck and meal. What's more, the self-styled Steven Kieran Dee was the persistent subject of his mother's over-weaning ways, evidenced by the fact that a consignment of clean clothes (and probably cash) arrived weekly c/o The Dublin Poetry Collective. Skiddy was moving in. Biscuits today. What would it be tomorrow?
   - Who in Jaysus' name is Jenkins?
Jack demanded in an absent-minded way, still observing the painstaking almost imperceptible progress of the scaffolder along the footpath below. Rosa raised an eye-brow at the aggressive tone in his voice as she passed. He knew it didn't become him and that Skiddy had successfully provoked him.

Skiddy re-entered, burning himself off the tea-pot which he carried awkwardly, the door held open by Arlene. Skiddy smiled seductively at Arlene. Arlene blushed then cowered at Jack's accusing eyes for she knew that the meeting to come was to deal with the financial crisis which she as Accounts Clerk to the Poetry Collective had failed to predict. Jack quietly rued the day they had been prevailed upon by Jobquest to take on Arlene to do their accounts in return for some measly employment grant. Aside from only later realising her tendency to burst into tears at the mildest of harsh words she was also not an Accounts Clerk of any sort. Thank you Jobquest, very much. Jack eased his tone. After all, Arlene was as much a victim of Jobquest and their sly manipulation of the live register figures as they. It was either the collective or the disability register for Arlene.
   - Who Arlene?
She stared at him in disbelief. How could Jack be so unenlightened?
   - Professor Jenkins, Jack.
Skiddy laughed lustily at Jack's growing impatience. Arlene blushed as the tremor of his laugh passed through her body. Rosa, aware of Jack's exasperation with Arlene and aware too that the woman had forgotten to take her medication that day, intervened.
   - Do you mind not standing there? Jenkins will be here any minute.
It was only then that Jack recognised the name of Rosa's former English professor. He was both relieved and suspicious given the same character's penchant for the company of his female students.
   - What does he want?

Rosa just shook her head. She was in a bad mood with him. He decided not to persist, not least because a commanding double-knock on the hall door now reverberated through the Hi Brasil and they all stopped as if in a game of musical chairs. Skiddy slid into the seat beside the heater, warmly observing the tension between Jack and Rosa as Arlene sprung into hostess mode. The others busily polished off the biscuits, Jack's biscuits. He couldn't think what he had done to annoy Rosa, a person who didn't even let her period get to her. Perhaps she had heard those lone horses bridling at the bit as he sped up O'Connell Street.

Like a hysterical and precocious child Professor Paddy Jenkins glided into the room, hands firmly planted in the deep pockets of his fashionable woollen overcoat and hand-knit scarf thrown over one shoulder de-noting perennial student image. Lifting his pockets, he spread his woollen wings in the sacred space that Rosa's cleaning operation had opened up. Turning to look upon their expectant faces he suddenly grew solemn. He savoured their attention while eyeing each of them.
     - Poets, friends and former alumnae, this is a sad day for poetry.
As far as Jack was concerned, it couldn't get much sadder.
     - The time to mourn has arrived. Poets the world over, the people of Ireland, of the County Kilkenny communities of Castlecomer and Moneen Roe are tonight mourning the passing of one of our true giants.

Jack knew immediately to whom he referred. Word of illness had reached them from London, death so imminent he had considered stalling publication of the Bulletin.
     - Meaney!
The name fell from his lips and all eyes turned on Jack. Some of them were clearly in the dark awaiting enlightenment. However, Jack had spent a good slice of his youth in the desolate north Kilkenny uplands where Martin Meaney had been reared. Jenkins looked at him gratefully as if Jack had spared him having to utter the unspeakable. He appeared to emit an involuntary whimper.
     - Is dead.
Another might construe his involuntary emission as a giggle of delight. He quickly suppressed this emotion, dropping his head into a prayerful silence as the poets, some of whom clearly did not recognise the dead poet's name, exchanged looks that varied from Jack's growing circumspection of their guest, Skiddy's sulking indifference, Rosa's

searching stare and big wet tears from Arlene who was already blessing herself and commencing the rosary.

- My friends, Poetry must act and be seen to act in recognition of this towering figure of our times.

Jack's clouded mind could only think of the scaffolder who he had left lying on the pavement. Meaney could not be saved but this poor character could. He should have acted then, but Jenkins was now commanding their attention with an urgent and businesslike manner. A memorial medal was in the process of being minted in the Kilkenny foundry where the tools that Martin Meaney had used as a miner were made. The medal would be awarded to the author of a commemorative poem in Meaney's honour. Jenkins appeared uncertain in the face of their hungry disinterested stares. He cleared his throat commandingly.

- There will of course be a financial consideration for the writer of the winning poem.

- How much?

Skiddy was first to stake his claim. Jack noticed Jenkins' sly cold smile at this demonstration of poet hunger.

- One thousand pounds.

He had their attention. Jack, seeing Skiddy's hunger bared, realised events were moving apace. He watched the eyes of the down-at-heel poets sizing each other up. Jack was dubious, not least because Meaney was not yet cold in his grave. He cleared his throat, an indication that the meeting should be called to order.

- Welcome, Professor Jenkins. The meeting joins with you in solidarity at the news of the death of a great poet and revolutionary.

Jenkins face broke into a weak smile. Jack's acceptance or otherwise of him was immaterial. Jack continued.

- The meeting would at this early stage like to indicate to the Professor that The Dublin Poetry Collective has a policy on prizes.

The combined gathering set their anxious eyes on Jack.

- In principal we are against them, as competition among members is contrary to our collective purpose and merely breeds dissent.

- Even if it is good for poetry?

Jenkins retorted smugly to nods of approval from a far too numerous band of poets for Jack to win a vote. Time to lay down the law.

- I refer to Section 5 Sub-section 2a of our constitution, which states that the proceeds of all prizes and bursaries secured by committee members shall be allocated to the collective aims of the organisation.

Jenkins seemed surprised but not affronted.

- Of course! You're a collective.

Jenkins appeared to be preparing to leave or change the subject. Skiddy seemed deflated. Jack should have left it at that, but struck out for the high moral ground, feeling the ghost of Meaney standing by his side.

- Anyway poetry is not about winners and losers.
- Bullshit!

Skiddy intervened.

- Talent must out.

Jack ignored him.

- Meaney was a communist, Professor Jenkins?
- Here we go.

Skiddy scoffed, ignored by Jack.

- ...and did not believe in setting poet against poet.

Skiddy was now glaring at him as if Jack had denied him his birthright.

- Either we're a collective or we are not.

Jack's voice hit falsetto, recent pressures finally finding voice.

- Afraid you won't win, comrade. Huh?

Jack didn't know how to respond to this so he ignored the comment. He noticed the others, including Rosa, recoiling from the fray. Skiddy railed.

- I propose we scrap that little communistic sub-clause of yours and let the best man win.

Skiddy scanned the other poets who didn't wish to get drawn in.

- I second that!

Arlene burst in out of nowhere, startling even Skiddy.

Jack looked at the other poets and then at Rosa, only then remembering her associate membership status precluded her participation as she was after all not a poet. Anyway, she had no time for his communist beliefs and they had long agreed to stop converting each other to their respective world views.

- Or woman.

A lone Kate Keane stood in the shadow of the doorway. The whole room – Jenkins slower than the others – turned to look at the source of this crucial intervention. Kate Keane strode across the creaking floorboards, watched by a suspicious Professor Jenkins. If they already knew each other Kate did her best to pretend otherwise.

- Martin Meaney is not even buried and ye're preparing to plunder his legacy.

More than that Kate Keane didn't elaborate, but there was conviction, even resentment, in the way she expressed herself. As the others were not to be drawn into taking sides, it was stalemate. A bruised and confused Paddy Jenkins grew silent, and took to scrutinising Kate

Keane, who ignored him. Always in search of compromise, Jack proposed the adjournment of the matter to a newly formed "Sub-Committee on Policy, Procedures and Prizes".

- Suit yourself!

Was all that could be heard from Skiddy as he slammed the door behind him. Jenkins took this as his cue to leave, edging away from Kate Keane's hostile glances with promises to remain in close communication.

An air of deflation suffused the room. Jack felt the pall of blame descend on him and fell to listening as Arlene outlined the paltry sales figures for the last issue of the Monthly Poetry Bulletin. They would not make the necessary inroads in their printing debt, so there was method in Jack's laying down of matters constitutional. One thousand pounds - the prize on offer - was precisely the amount owed by the Collective to their former printer who had threatened to sell their debt to a loan-shark. Jack wanted to argue that if they stuck together, they could collectively write The Poetry Collective out of debt by one or another of them seizing this Meaney Money. However, the members were already counting the coppers in their pockets in anticipation of a pint in Conway's or were slipping away for sneaky smokes in the corridor. He decided to let the matter lie.

By the time he adjourned the meeting, the torrential rain had ceased. The Square was now in silence and the scaffolder had departed or had been swept away into the city drains by the torrent. Why had the man been so insistent with Jack on the matter of his profession? So what if he was a scaffolder. Would he have proffered this information to any enquiring passer-by? By the time Jack had turned back from his musings to say his goodbyes the room behind him had emptied.

II
The Id In Skiddy

- I believe you know Sam Beckett?

Professor Paddy Jenkins turned on his heel with nothing like the style he had demonstrated to the meeting and looked at the young man addressing him in such familiar terms with scant recognition even though it was only five minutes since they had parted company. Skiddy knew a narcissist when he saw one and prided himself on the timing of his ambush, on the traffic island corner of Parnell Street and Square. Jenkins looked surprisingly spooked. Maybe he thought Skiddy was some knacker about to mug him.

- Well yes in fact I have had the acquaintance of Mister Beckett.

Skiddy was aware from press reports of the Beckett biography in hand.

- Of all your books, this sounds the most promising.

- It does?

Jenkins was clearly not used to being summed up by one of such youth and low standing in the world of poetry. Skiddy had to watch his step. Jenkins looked anxious for the green man to let him off the island in the direction of the Gate Theatre where he was to attend a pre-performance drinks reception for the celebrated author of Jaded! a West End hit the London critics had hailed as a masterpiece of political satire and which was now being rolled out to provincial outlets. Jenkins feared in the tendencious title a diatribe against a failing leader for whom he held a creeping if unfashionable regard. For reasons of profile he needed to attend. The premature resolution of the bizarre affair he had just escaped had left him in a quandary: run the gauntlet of drug addicts and general undesirables on O'Connell Street back to Trinity or arrive unfashionably early for the reception? Suddenly, the entreaties of this insolent youth to enter Conway's Public House appeared attractive.

- I'd say he's a cranky get. You'd have to be to write with that spleen.

- Excuse me?

- Beckett?

- Au contraire. One must not confuse the artist with the art.

Spare me that duality nonsense, Skiddy thought, and considered saying so when the prowling bar-man caught his eye at 20 paces.

He couldn't help notice how shy of this same contact the well-heeled professor proved. Never mind. Skiddy would be paid the morrow for the hatchet job on the tax-dodging property hoarding proprietors of the poetry collective building. "The Ceaucescus of Georgiana" he had dubbed the unwitting Overend family. Serves them fucking right.

Perhaps he had primed Jenkins too well with the Beckett prompt. The man didn't draw breath on the subject of Beckett for another 15 minutes, nor did he drink very much, which was even more worrying because Skiddy was down to the dregs. He realised he needed to be a little more attentive and this distracted him from the pint issue. The more he listened the better the idea he was getting about the mind-set of Professor Jenkins who he was damn sure, despite mention of "a jury of eminent professionals", would be the final arbiter of the Martin Meaney Memorial Medal+Money.

He took Jenkins for a frustrated poet, a dabbler perhaps, who used academia to live the artistic life vicariously and without the pain of poverty. Or maybe he was one of these smart-arses who believed that Joyce had said it all so why bother. If you couldn't construct, you could de-construct what others had so painstakingly and mysteriously constructed. These critics and academics supported each other and believed themselves on a par with those they wrote about. The pedestal on which the artist had once been elevated turned to rubble at the hands of these academics and critics, most of them frustrated artists determined to de-mystify and diminish what they didn't have themselves. Talent.

Skiddy reckoned Jenkins was a pseudo-lefty type, that he was probably well into this post-modernist guff that was so much in vogue with the 1968 generation. The winning poem for this Meaney Medal would need a touch of social conscience, not too heavy on the racial anger he felt coursing through his west of Ireland veins in a way that none of that crowd in the Collective could match. Skiddy could give them the absurdism of Beckett mixed with the brooding emotions of McGahern. He himself had been reared in the town of Galway but he loved all that bucolic stuff. That was the real Ireland. This we-must-look-to-Europe mantra being pedalled by the country's Poetry Establishment was pulling the race away from the elemental mad fucking and fighting hoors of old. But might his winning recipe not also result in some post-modernist pot pourri? So what? If it worked who gave a fuck? At this point in his career, he needed to bag an award.

A poet, Skiddy believed, above all things needed a persona if he was to rise above the heap. Look at the soon-to-be-interred Martin Meaney. Revolutionary antics and a reputation for sleeping with other men's wives had made his name. Not his average poetry and minor output. Under the umbrella of derring-do and sexual notoriety Meaney had managed to conceal his average work. Who would be brave enough to stand up and say this over the mournful chorus of lament the poet's passing would evoke in the coming days? That said, you had to give the fucker credit. He was a man ahead of his time. The artist Meaney was the art. Let's face it, the communist utopian dream might be up but revolutionary antics were better than no antics.

In a very short space of time S.K Dee too had carved a name for himself about the town. His output minimal, he nonetheless had artist written all over him. He had every belief the art would follow. In the meantime, courting Jenkins and whatever grandees of the Dublin Literary Scene crossed his path was part of the campaign to make his mark. If he kept it together he could be sure that by the time his entry for the Meaney Medal had landed on Jenkins' desk he would have stirred The Professor's king-making inclinations.

Cynical? I'll give you cynical. This Festschrift which would include the winning poem was nothing but an elaborate career move by Paddy Jenkins. The signing up of the so-called up-and-coming talent that lurked around the Collective was all a bit of street credibility, a fig leaf for a you-scratch-my-back-I'll-scratch-yours exercise in self-promotion being charged on the account of the deceased. But why pick on Meaney, a poet who had dwelt in relative obscurity in life and probably deserved to remain there in death? Had the man's passing that day inspired a sudden reappraisal? What was in it for Jenkins? Skiddy wondered if Jenkins' Beckett biography had stalled. Perhaps the Fox of Foxrock had rumbled Jenkins as a chancer despite his Trinity credentials and had given him a royal kick up the Boulevard Montparnasse.

Jenkins' ambulance chasing instincts would have brought the poor medical reports about Martin Meaney to his notice and he would have lain in wait for the inevitable in the belief that dead poets were a safer bet than the live and unpredictable. A dead poet was a rare commodity these days. They weren't dying fast enough. Greater longevity, state pensions, celebrity status, and American university sinecures were ensuring longevity. The newer generation of poets weren't destroying themselves at the same speed as the last. Where were the new hell-raisers, the larger than life characters that the biographers thrived on?

The Martin Meaney Memorial Medal was probably just the tip of an emerging venture that would include a summer school in the poet's home-village of Moneen Roe where visiting dons wearing silly sun hats would tutor the premium-paying US students with great tits and loosened morals. Invites to bring his Meaney show across the Atlantic would follow. Jenkins would break into America on the back of Meaney. Then would follow the definitive biography, considered reviews by his buddies in the Irish Times, radio and tv profiles, not to mention money. Above all, Meaney represented an escape for Jenkins from the thing he resented most. Teaching. He wanted to be a player. Or so Skiddy thought in the rush of beer to the head.

He was not only now bored senseless by the name-dropping that had ensued, but was pondering an empty glass. Conway's was filling up with Sinn Féiners. A flag-waving football crowd was descending too for some pre-European Cup warm up match. Those useless long-faced fuckers from the Poetry Collective would soon be sliding through the door counting their pennies. Jenkins was looking uncomfortable amidst the panoply of Easter lillies, black arm-bands, moustached faces, bad colour-co-ordination, loud Northern accents mixing with long low and conspiratorial drawling Dublin vowels. Time to take charge.

As they strolled along the railings of the Rotunda, watched by a couple of teen-age junkies, Jenkins appeared grateful for Skiddy's initiative in leading the exit. The Professor turned the conversation to The Poetry Collective. Skiddy knew he had to be careful not to run his fellow poets down, directly, so he looked Jenkins in the eye.
    - Collectives don't write great poetry, Professor Jenkins. Some people would prefer to have endless meetings about procedure. This motion that motion. I'm more for e-motion myself.
    - Well the Monthly Poetry Bulletin is rather a fine production. That Jack-what's-his-name seems to have put his heart into it.
Exactly where Skiddy didn't want the conversation to drift.
    - Well he gets a lot of help from the rest of us mere mortals Professor, and especially from his girlfriend Rosa.
    - I see, they're an item.
Not for long, if Skiddy could help it.
    - Rosa is an ex-student of mine, don't you know. A very fine student.

This appeared to suggest some ownership that might supersede Jack's. Skiddy wondered if he'd ever tried it on with her in a tutorial.

- I'm disappointed she hasn't made the break into writing her own work. A waste to see her standing behind a shop-counter all day. On her knees more like it, Skiddy thought. Wasted on Karl Bollix Marx too.

- Yes, Professor but she has other talents and talent will out. Jenkins had not missed the double-entendre and looked at Skiddy knowingly. Now they were co-conspirators. Let's just bury the annoying communist swiftly.

- In fact Professor, she's the one who really deserves the credit for keeping our little show on the road.

- She's quite a girl!
Jenkins' next words came like music to Skiddy's ears.

- Now, tell me about yourself! Is that a west of Ireland brogue I detect there?
Professor Jenkins had touched on two subjects very close to Skiddy's heart. Himself and The West of Ireland. Perhaps it was the rush of Jenkins' dregs to the head while the Don relieved himself in the John, or the lack of food in his system, but Skiddy found himself rising a little too enthusiastically to the invitation.

He told Jenkins how much a stranger he felt in Dublin, this city of the coloniser, and how much more at home he felt with the cadences and rhythms of the west. There was nothing he liked better than to exchange curses with the boatmen along the Claddagh or on Spiddal Pier.

- I see, you have The Gaelic?
- The font of our poetic voice, Professor.
He lied, knowing he was in the company of a West Brit and that his ignorance of their native tongue would not be detected.

- And are you writing in Gaelic?
The Professor asked somewhat in awe.

- Not at the moment. It's more that I'm excavating what I see are the tensions between the old language and the English, between East and West if you like. It's providing an exciting seam of tension in the work.

As a biographer Skiddy knew that Jenkins would pick up on the signifiers of poetic promise. Exile. Internal Exile. Internal conflict (his mother from the Gaeltacht, his father from the Galltacht). Fuck it, a love of conversation and the elixir of alcohol. Jenkins seemed impressed.

Skiddy observed from the proliferation of taxis pulling up under the gaze of Parnell and spewing out their dolled up middle aged ladies and long coated bucks with big gouty guts, that Jenkins was about to be re-united with his tribe after his detour into the wild side. Before Jenkins could dismiss him, Skiddy held out his hand in a manly fashion and drew the Professor close.

- Meaney would be proud of you, Sir.

Jenkins looked both surprised and moved by the encouragement.

- Why thank you...

Yes, he had already forgotten Skiddy's name. Narcissist.

- S.K. Dee. Steven Kieran Dee.
- Thank you, Steven ...
- SK will do fine.

Skiddy looked up the street in the direction of the gathering hoi polloi.

- Now go and convince them!
- Yes, indeed I shall.

A bewildered Jenkins dutifully sidled off.

- That's better!

Make these fucking cultural apparatchiks work for the artist and not the other way round, Skiddy surmised as he watched Jenkins join some high spirited toffee-nosed fellow west Brit. He raised a celebratory cigarette to his mouth and sucked off it. He was pondering whether to go back to his digs to commence his entry for the Meaney Medal when he noticed the down-and-out sitting against the railings, scrutinising him. Was he about to be hustled for a fag? The cadger was gazing at him with searing eyes. Get the retaliation in first.

- Get your own, loser.

The man seemed unfazed by the order and continued to stare at Skiddy through glazed eyes.

- Even a serpent cannot ascend a slippery pole, Sir.

Skiddy didn't like the sound of this. He looked at the half-finished cigarette and with characteristic disdain stepped closer and shoved it in the man's face. The man appeared not to see it, but continued to stare Skiddy down.

- Suit yourself, old timer!

Skiddy retorted from a safe distance. His words appeared to be deflected by the guy's heavy energy focused on him. He was so freaked out by the bad vibes that he continued to back out into the street without a care for the traffic. A cold sweat shot down his body as he dodged through the theatre time taxis and buses. From the safety of the other side he looked back over his shoulder to make sure the hobo wasn't coming after him. The mucker was nowhere to be seen. Unfuckingreal.

By closing time, Skiddy was firmly ensconced in The Long Hall expounding on the poverty of contemporary Irish poetry like he was the man who would single-handedly lead the revival. His fellow poets seemed prepared to let him off uninterrupted so he took the opportunity to prime them on the coming Policy, Procedures and Prize-money show-down with Jack. Could they really allow for a regime of mediocrity to reign through Karl Bollix Marx all-for-one strategy? All appeared to shake their heads in agreement. Talent Must Prevail.

He'd be doing Jack a favour. Skiddy was convinced that the little poetry virgin needed to be woken up to the pain of loss, somehow. His holier-than-thou attitudes needed to be cut from under him. Less Marx more Nietzsche for him from now on. A poet needed a sense of loss, a well of pain from which to distil his art. What Skiddy wouldn't do to have a really tragic past, instead of always having to invent one, or even borrow one. He remembered the night in Galway he had employed Jack's story as his own to get a girl into bed. He had her in tears. Well someone had to make use of that tragedy if Jack wouldn't. This after all was the age of the counterfeiter. Originality in the artist, not the art.

III
Night Writing

Rosa's expectations about the visit of her Professor Jenkins to the poetry collective had been flattened by the unseemly row about procedure that had ended the meeting. Was it the solidarity Kate Keane had shown Jack? Or Rosa's powerlessness due to her lack of status as a poet? Or the pointless argument between Jack and Skiddy, when Jack knew that Skiddy would do his own thing anyway?

She walked slowly down the broad stairs of this brooding house that had once served as a hotel for visitors from the countryside. She peered into Room 9, their bedroom. Jack listened attentively to his cassette recorder using headphones. To what, she didn't know. There was something furtive about his behaviour. Was he already preparing his piece for the Martin Meaney Medal, despite his stalling efforts at the meeting? She stepped back into the shadows as he stopped transcribing. Did he sense her presence? She watched as he let out a laugh, shook his head in apparent disbelief and started to write again. Was he laughing at her? Was he trying to make her jealous by showing how well his work had been going? Was he aware that she was spying on him? She wished he were, for the idea that he was having a good time on his own filled her with jealousy.

When Jack finally fell into bed beside her, sleep did not come easily and both lay there in silence listening to Conway's empty, the last bus filling over the sound of racing engines on the square before setting off into the far-strewn satellites of Finglas, Swords and Skerries. They both wished for sleep, Jack because he wanted to banish that voice in the tape that had filled the evening hours. Live in the moment, he heard a voice say. Reach out and take her in your arms. Take her in your arms he heard the order of a stranger's voice. A lone horse travels faster another voice came. Half asleep he was already travelling, his mind leading his body back through the day, the relentless queue in Cumberland Street Dole office, the urchin slipping him the tape bearing Terry Crowe's life-story, up and down the hollow stairs to the printers shop, cajoling Red Ink to meet the 5.30 deadline, the repeated thud of the stapler on the spine of the magazine, the near miss with the clerk on O'Connell Bridge, the scaffolder, the scaffolder. Where had he come from? Where was he now? Hopefully not a similar fate to poor

Martin Meaney. A lonely death in London after a life of solidarity. He felt Rosa move closer to him, but all he could think of was Martin Meaney's cold decaying body. The suck of the grave. His body felt cold from the draught he had been sitting in all evening. This body could not promise Rosa much warmth. Feigning sleep, he rolled over and buried his head in the pillow.

For Rosa, sleep did not come. By drawing closer to Jack she had tried to climb on the wave that had taken him but she was becalmed and soon all the noises of the old hotel were becoming exaggerated, the cries of the drunks on the street more desperate, a couple in the neighbouring B 'n' B making love to a soundtrack of match highlights and We are The Champions booming out of a ghetto-blaster.

Rosa too had things on her mind. Not just the fact that she and Jack had not made love for three long winter months, New Years Eve in fact, three cycles unmarked. She was convinced that their house had been the subject of an uninvited intrusion. Furniture had been moved inexplicably; windows clumsily left open; and an alien odour mixed with the tapestry of scents of the old hotel, spices and coffee from their kitchen, coconut oil and detergent from the bathroom, damp stored in the walls and the piles of unsold poetry bulletins in the hallway below. This was a new and pervasive smell, a body odour she could not identify in any of the living occupants and visitors to the house. It was evidence to her of an unwelcome intrusion. She had wanted to bring it to Jack's attention but he had been so engaged in other things it had not been possible.

Intrusion was probably too strong a word. This was evidence of a disturbance which she believed had a psychic or perhaps paranormal basis. She was convinced that this same force was targeting Jack, as its appearance had coincided with a change in his behaviour. She needed to tell him, but was afraid of accusations of superstition, or "your mumbo jumbo" as he liked to call it. He needed to be told soon.

Long after the couple next door had collapsed into post-coital bliss, leaving the stage to Freddy Mercury's irksome falsetto, Rosa remained listening to Jack breathe and when sometime later he turned in his sleep and let out a low laugh she had had enough and slipped from the bed in search of some peace in the now silent and abandoned hulk of the hotel.

On her perch in the kitchen she opened her notebook. She observed the progress made over previous nights and how these words, written in states of near exhaustion, were making some sense to her. The banging of the window in the hallway and the low whistle of wind coming up the stairs reminded her of her purpose. If last night's events were to be repeated she would not have long to wait. She flicked back through the pages to remind herself of these phenomena: on Monday she had noticed a roof-window half open; the following night the fire-escape door had been left off the latch. When she had asked Jack if he was responsible for these he had denied it. She had no reason not to believe him. On Wednesday she noticed the aforementioned body odour. Finally there was last night's apparition and confirmation for her that Jack was the target of these spirits.

Rosa had been woken up by a banging on the front-door. Presuming it to be one of the collective members stranded in town having missed the last bus she went to answer it and found it already unlocked from within. She called out to whoever had knocked. Receiving no answer, she had cautiously opened the door. Standing naked in the shadows, shivering and still asleep and reciting some gibberish, which she could not decipher, she found Jack. She had presumed him sleeping beside her in their bed. She had never seen him in this state before. Naked yes, but not like this.

Returning him to bed up the flights of stairs he had fallen asleep in her arms. Unable to sleep she passed the following hours absorbing the image he had presented to her on the front step. Half awake half asleep she began to question whether it was real or imagined. Could it have been the play of the street lights creating shadows or the effects of the freezing night on his now non existent protuberance? Was she hallucinating? Of course not. This appearance was confirmation of that instinct she had had at first sighting him two years before. That appearance, like this one, had borne all the marks of a visitation.

To another the sight that confronted her would have come as a shock in its defiance of nature. For her it represented a kind of Second Coming and it confirmed her belief in him as being other than human. Not only did the Jack who confronted her at the front door of their house have two heads, that of a man and a woman, but where his penis should have been there was only a mound of hair. She had only previously seen illustrations of this ancient form in dusty manuals but here was a living manifestation.

Rosa now had the clearest confirmation yet of what she had long suspected: that her partner Jack, her deepest and first love was in fact a hermaphrodite. Whoever these spirits were that had taken possession of the house, they were drawing him further towards his self-realisation, towards his revelation. She needed to tell him. Perhaps he already knew he was a hermaphrodite and had succeeded in concealing it from most, if not her. If he was unaware of this state, he would reject the suggestion and think less of her. He might think she was portraying him as some sexual freak, which she wasn't. What she believed she had witnessed on their door-step was the spirit made flesh.

Tiredness, she knew, could beguile and she had to allow for the slimmest possibility that she had imagined it all. However, this apparition was for her the confirmation of what she had long-suspected. She only needed to find the way to communicate to Jack what she firmly believed, in a way that would make him recognise himself while not thinking any less of her.

Rosa Nugent worked in The Alchemist's Head bookshop on Essex Street, a back-water street of a backwater city in a backwater country. On graduating with a degree in Pure English from Trinity College a couple of years previously she had commenced working in the shop part-time. The shop specialised in The Occult, Astrology, the Magic Arts. With the emergence of what were being fashionably termed New Age philosophies it had been opening its shelves to books on the subjects of Healing and Alternative medicines of different kinds. The Alchemist's Head was more than a shop. It was an axis for spiritualists and witches and Rosa's friends, those few of the class of 1985 who hadn't opted for emigration.

Sitting by the window with her friend Janette musing on the infrequent passers-by on No-Sex Street as Janette preferred to call it, she noticed a young man exit the premises of The Communist Party of Ireland bookshop across the road. He seemed to be possessed of an intense excitement or enthusiasm, in a hurry to his next port of call, eyes already on the horizon before he had even climbed on his bike, an action which he managed however with dexterity. Rosa recognised a mercurial energy and an awareness that allowed him to look both ways at once. Janette identified in his exaggerated gestures, pursed lips and the feminine way he hung his head "an even money wager for a poufe".

27

Rosa kept her counsel but not enough to feign disinterest. What interested her was that quality Janette misconstrued as homosexuality but that Rosa identified as the mark of Androgyny. Even at this early stage she suspected that the young man in her sights was in fact a hermaphrodite.

She would see him pass regularly up A-Sex Street (as she soon re-named it in his honour) his energy at odds with the slothful city, perhaps because he received his energy from elsewhere. One day she turned from her reading of the I Ching to see him staring at her through the front window of the shop. In fact he wasn't staring at her. He was trying to read an acetate notice advertising a course in Psychic Healing and had not seen her in the comparative shadow of the shop interior. This had allowed her to look closer, into his eyes, into his head, where she could see his thoughts and an expression that turned from scepticism to embarrassment as a passing bread van bounced light onto her face and revealed them to the other's gazing eyes. He blinked, blushed and then he was gone.

A week later he was in the shop asking if he could put up a poster for "An Evening Of African Nationalist Poetry". Unfortunately Janette was there too and decided to make fun of him behind his back by mimicking his expressions of scepticism at the shop's cultish fare. Rosa noticed that although he lingered to look at the books he never picked any up. She presumed that as a communist he disapproved of the Occult as mere False Consciousness and that to touch would be contaminating. He wouldn't have been the first superstitious communist. Stalin had been as dependent on Astrology as he had on the principles of Historical Materialism. Jack would later counter with dismissals of Stalin's interest in Astrology as being consistent with his deviant personality and remind her of much more current disciples "of this mumbo-jumbo", namely Nancy and Ronald Reagan.

She soon learned that he was known about the place as Jack. In these early encounters the only word he ever spoke was "Can?" as he requested permission to put up a poster on the shop notice-board. Not "Can I?", just "Can?" The "I" deemed irrelevant, the executor of the action of putting the poster on the wall completely secondary to the action. This lack of apparent ego was attractive as she had become bored with the egoism of the young men she had come to know through university. These objections had proscribed her to the most fleeting relationships pursued for the mere purposes of sexual gratification. Having graduated a year before, she had traded these scant offerings for a life of celibacy on No-Sex Street and had become pessimistic about ever finding love.

Despite this lack of communication between them she had already deduced that he was an Air sign, attractive to her as a Virgo but which she knew would make him eternally elusive. This was already the most unusual and elusive of courtships, which went like this.

Jack would make a point of advertising the events he was organising in the shop and she would turn up at these events, a series of poetry readings, protests and political debates. He would behave as if they had not met before, but make a point of passing her when gathering donations at the end of the evening, or looking for signatories for a letter of protest. Either he was very shy or was making her prove her worthiness. She made a lot of donations to causes she knew very little about. She signed many petitions, never failing to include her phone number with her address. The Special Branch called, but he never did.

Then he was gone. No bicycle rattling off the cobblestones. No posters. No Jack. She became so desperate to see him as the days and then the weeks passed that she would cross Essex Street to the Communist Party bookshop and make up some story about a fuse having blown in their kettle or the water being turned off on their side of the street. While waiting for the comrades' kettle to boil she would read their notice-board and decide on the most likely event at which to locate him. Previously exciting political gatherings condemning British repressive measures in The North or US imperialism everywhere became dreary and hopeless events as he failed to materialise. She became deeply pessimistic and depressed about the future of the world and presumed that Jack had emigrated as had most of their generation or had followed the trail of other communist romantics on a six-month stint to Latin America.

This courtship, in which she was in no doubt that he was thinking about her, was defined more by absence than any tangible communication. Though they were destined to finally meet, it was this quality of non-communication and absence that would describe their relationship. She had in the meantime learned his full name and through an enquiry to the University College Dublin Registration Office, posing as a prospective employer, confirmed his date and place of birth. Posing as a medical research student she gained access to the files of the National Maternity Hospital where she ascertained his exact time of birth.

Through October and November she busied herself drawing up his astrological chart. The hermaphrodite is "conceived in the bath (or a watery bed perhaps) born in the air" (M Maier Atalanta Fugiens, Oppenheim 1618). She grew to understand the self-contained nature of his existence and that "the hermaphrodite, lying in the dark like a corpse, needs fire." This suggested that all the battles in which he was involved over Nicaragua, Northern Ireland and on behalf of the North-side Street Traders were not only about changing the world but were the fires of conflict from which the tincture of his nascent creativity were being distilled.

Rosa was certain that the young man she had fallen for was a hermaphodite. While she confided this to no one she did make the mistake of asking Janette if she had seen him about. Janette was delighted to hear Rosa express an interest in "the poufe". Rosa immediately regretted mentioning him as Janette had quickly cheapened her deepening emotions.

December came and Winter gnawed at her hope. His chart indicated a turn soon after his disappearance from her sphere. Definitely not another woman. There had been a death. Not his own, though it was clear his fire had gone out and his blood was cold. She envisioned a pair stretched out and mistook it initially as the hermaphrodite in its latent corpse like form. But it wasn't. Nor was it the twins of his birth sign either. Whoever it was, had passed. There it was in his chart. The sun and the moon of the hermaphrodite had been extinguished. She became further depressed. But this time it was out of concern for him, out of a love for him which she was gradually explaining to herself.

In the afternoon of the Winter Solstice Janette called to say that their gang were arriving back on the mail-boat on Christmas Eve and that they should make themselves available for a reunion. Now this for Rosa was the worst part of not being an emigrant. She put the engagement and all thought of turning up out of her mind. When days later she heard an overwrought squawk on Dame Street she mistook it for one of the sea-birds straying off the tidal river. "Over here fruitcake!" was Janette's way of enticing her in the direction of the Stag's Head. There was no escape.

The pub was brimming with drunken exiles, but she heard him before she saw him. He was in the throes of some political discourse with one of the Gang. She pushed through the throng. He looked at her in stunned recognition, but didn't cease talking, Hermes and Aphrodite working in unison as he continued bombarding Janette's London squeeze Gerry for abandoning the cause. More words from him in three seconds than in the whole three months of their silent courtship.

"Jesus, it's your poufe," Janette spat in her ear as they sidled into the bar. He looks different Rosa thought, thinner, more drawn. His chart had been correct. His sun and moon had waned for a period, but he appeared to be waxing again. She turned from the bar to observe him and found him staring at her. Right again. He had been thinking of her during those months out of alignment, wherever he had been?

Gerry and Janette dominated the conversation with their tales of summer in London, swimming naked in the Serpentine, all laced with plenty of innuendo, a menu of gigs with bands who never made it to recession-hit Dublin, defying council evictions in the wake of the Greater London Council's demise. Their flirting soon gave way to petting. Gerry and Janette were clearly preparing to fuck each other's brains out as soon as they possibly could. And all the time Rosa and Jack remained dutifully silent spectators until Janette, picking up on their silence, turned to Jack.
- Have you moved to London as well? We haven't seen you around much lately.
Gerry quickly burst in.
- You must be joking. It's either do Dublin or die for Jack.
- A bit too fond of the apron strings?
Janette intervened.
Jack tensed at this point. Gerry too.
- Steady on girl!
Janette who had always had a problem being heard among the smarter and self-confident gang didn't like being censored.
- What's his problem?
Then turning to Jack.
- What's your problem?
She was becoming mildly hysterical.
- Problem?
Gerry was looking at Janette with different eyes.
- Yeh problem.
Janette had not understood Rosa's attraction to Jack. In fact she was

convinced that not only was Jack a poufe but that Rosa was a lesbian. Gerry seemed spooked.

- I think you might be projecting a little bit there lady.

Janette had waltzed casually out of college into employment with the aid of some family connection in Advertising.

- What's that supposed to mean?
- There are no fucking apron strings, Gannet!

Janette recoiled at this corruption of her name.

- The guy must have come from somewhere.

Janette liked to play at being her own woman. Gerry for his part was finding this relationship thing tough, having cast Gannet as a summer shag to be picked up and dropped again. He looked at his empty glass and uttered something like "this fucking country". Then he threw his arms in the air, stood up and looked at the bar. Janette looked at him as if to say how dare you leave. So he turned and told her what she needed to know.

- They're gone, you know. The guy's folks just died. Happy?

Rosa thought Gerry said this like he was the one who had been hard done by in the tragedy, the simplicity of his plans for Janette torpedoed by her stupidity. Janette was now speechless. She looked at Rosa who was looking at Jack. Rosa wanted to shoot her. Then Janette squealed.

- I'm...oh my God!

Then looking after Gerry.

- Gerry?!

Jack was looking at the bar where Gerry had sought the cover of the gang from where the words "mad bitch" were emanating. Rosa was thinking how this nicely balanced Janette's earlier "fruitcake" salute across Dame Street when she was drawn by his voice.

- That's OK!

Jack was looking at Janette with sympathy.

- You weren't to know.

But it was as if the self-centred Janette didn't hear as she sought solace from Rosa.

- Rosa I'm really really...you know. God, the poor guy, both of them, he's so...nice.

"Sorry" was not a word in Janette's vocabulary and Rosa was already placing a spell on what had been a tenuous friendship based on their shared feelings of abandonment by their college tribe.

Janette kept staring at Rosa, but Rosa would not shift her gaze from Jack who was staring sympathetically at Janette. Realising that Gerry was not returning in a hurry Janette let out a further squeal and

32

evacuated her seat in favour of a proper weep in the bog. Jack followed her trail with what Rosa believed was a look of remarkable empathy given the "mad bitch's" insensitivity.

- Is your friend alright?

That was nice, she thought initially, but there was something in the way he said "friend" that made her feel like he was judging her. She wanted to explain that she was only with her "friend" because she was looking for him. She reached for the nearest explanation.

- She's been drinking all day.

- Fuck her!

Was Gerry's response as he returned with a fresh round of drinks. Then Gerry looked at Rosa, casually regaining possession of his friend's story and casting himself as the honest bearer of the unspeakable truth. If Janette and she were an odd match she couldn't reconcile Jack with his friend.

- The guy's folks are driving out in the country two months ago, take a wrong turning into the canal, and it's adios. Can you believe it?

Rosa was tiring of Gerry's direct approach and how he seemed to have appropriated the tragedy of his friend's parents' death. So she said, still looking at Jack.

- Yes! I can.

After all, she had seen the pair lying side by side on a cold plinth in his chart. Jack looked at her. Gerry looked at Jack, then at Rosa, sensing a conspiracy.

- I take it you two know each other?

Rosa hoped Jack would say something to indicate their previous encounters but he didn't.

- This Fucking Town. Everyone is so fucking tight arsed and tight fucking lipped.

His rant complete, a touch of humility crept back into Gerry's deliberations. He looked at Rosa.

- Listen whoever you are, I just want you to know this guy is a fucking amazing bloke. A psychological, biological and political anomaly...so if you do know him you should get to know him better and if you're just taking the piss and don't know him, get to know him. You strike me as a valuable member of this godforsaken race.

Rosa didn't warm to being referred to in such specimen-like terms. She did however detect in Gerry a true depth of feeling towards his friend, clearly lacking in her relationship with Janette, so she decided not to ruin things by telling him she already knew all these odd and beautiful things about his friend, as it might take some explaining and she didn't want the term "fruitcake" attached to her again, particularly in Jack's company.

Janette resurfaced from the toilet and joined The Gang at the bar, afraid of returning to the company of her last remaining Dublin friend who she suspected of being a witch with evil powers of retaliation, as well as a lesbian. Gerry, sensing her vulnerability went over to prey, but was promptly taken by surprise by Janette's announcement that she was moving to London, expecting this would expedite her swift return to the bosom of the tribe. Now it was Gerry's turn to go silent.

Rosa was indifferent to the news and the attentions of the Gang to her prolonged conversation with Jack. She knew they were being talked about, but she didn't care, happy to finally have him to herself.
    - You're a writer, aren't you?
The idea seemed to trouble Jack.
    - Kind of...
    - Kind of?
    - We're a collective of people who write different things.
    - You're a collective? "The he, the she and the is of it?"
    - Sorry?
    - Joyce in Finnegan's Wake. Most writers are collectives in themselves.
    - Oh!
    - The luxury of a degree in Pure English.
She assured him in his lack of knowledge of The Wake.
    - I don't think you understand. We are a collective.
    - I understand perfectly.

They talked about Austin Clarke, Joyce, Neruda and Patrick Kavanagh and a name she had never heard before, that of Martin Meaney, a poet and Spanish Civil War veteran who was now a great age and ailing in London. He spoke about how all had excelled in the celebration of the common place. He sounded almost nostalgic for the difficult times through which these writers had lived. She wondered if he too was seeking a life of impossible struggle.

She said she was particularly fond of Neruda's more sensuous work about nature and love of nature, indeed the love between a man and a woman. He said that he hadn't paid much attention to this aspect and added demonstratively.

- You know, Neruda is the only writer to have won the Lenin and The Nobel Prize for Literature.
What this had to do with the value of Neruda's poetry she wasn't sure. Perhaps it was just another evasion on his part. Was he afraid of intimacy? Otherwise, could he be so blind to Neruda's love poetry? She suppressed her belief that the poet's place is ultimately with the self - and not with the people - and was rewarded when he asked her what other poets she liked. The conversation was only interrupted by the arrival of Gerry with more pints and the address of a house in Ranelagh where a party was planned.
- Glad to see things are moving along!
With a wink Gerry absolved his friend of any compunction to join them at the party and asked Jack for a key to The Hi Brasil as Gerry didn't think he'd make it out to "the folks" in suburbia tonight. 'Gannet' was obviously still on the menu.

Rosa and Jack didn't make it to the party. They took to the Yuletide streets, Jack wheeling his bike in an almost loving way, calmly negotiating the post-pub partum fast manifesting itself as a river of spilt drink, piss and angry tears.

In the solitude of these streets she wanted to be closer to him. She wanted to kiss him. But his bike separated them. She noticed how tightly he held the handle-bars as if he was about to make a getaway. Though they did not touch, she made a point of placing a hand on the bicycle in the belief this would communicate an intimacy, without scaring him off. As she removed her hand from the saddle he drew the bicycle towards himself and lifted it off the kerb onto the street. Then he threw his leg over it. Was winged Hermes preparing to depart? So it seemed, as he leaned down and flicked on the dynamo. She felt completely stranded as he kicked the pedal anti-clockwise into take off position. Would he dump her in exactly the same position Janette had found her, minding her own business? Only then did he turn to her with a beaming face that spoke more of hello than goodbye, his gaze quickly dropping to the cross-bar.
- Hop on!
Before accepting the invite she brought her lips close to his and was relieved to find him respond. They kissed. A full and proper kiss. Her errant knight had returned to claim her.

Despite the evasiveness Jack proved to be her finest lover yet. Making love to him was unusual as at times you could feel the mind detach from the body. At first Rosa was curious as to where he went, but in time she learned to wander off on her own path. She found pursuing her own path brought her to many interesting places that were not of her daily reality. At times he arrived to join her there. This sacred union was not just the consummation of their relationship but the first sublime experience of her adult life. It set her on the road to becoming what she never thought she could become. Until then she had been an observer of life, love and art, but now she was partaking.

From that day on, she was not just a shop-worker, not just a woman in love for the first time. Not just someone's lover. She had become a believer after a long spell of pessimism. She may not have had the work to prove it but in her own mind Rosa crossed the bridge that night on the way to becoming a poet. She had imagined herself in to his life and here he was, the living proof of her imagining. Jack was her first creation.

In the minutes after lovemaking they would lie there in silence awaiting the rejoining of body and spirit, their spirits cavorting above their tired bodies. Sleep lifted, the union of body and spirit would be complete and he would invariably come out with something very ordinary like "I have to collect some posters from the printers" which in no way betrayed wherever it was he had been in dreams. She thought to ask him, or that he might ask her, but he never did so neither did she. Like there were many things they never talked about. She valued this silence and preferred to imagine where he might have been rather than have him describe. He was a blank page she had been writing before they met and now that they had met she found herself no more enlightened by his silent ways and therefore felt further compelled to imagine.

Rosa awoke at the kitchen table. She realised she had been making love to him in a dream as she had made love to him for the first time and that unlike the first time she had fully climaxed. She hugged herself with the cold and the remnants of the climax passed through her body.

She closed her eyes to rejoin the dream that had brought her back from that first time they had made love, how she held him in her hands and guided him slowly into her. How once there he had stayed still for a time, caressed her face and not so much looked at her as through her. She had been shocked by the intensity, but now that she understood him she could remember it for its pleasure. She reached between her legs to aid the feeling back, then realised there was someone standing in the hall. She recognised the glinting eyes in the dark. Looking at her or through her?

Had she dreamed it from the bed to come and be with her, in that state that was neither alive or dead, asleep or awake? The light of the moon etched the dark side. The first light of the dawn filled his warmer face. His sex had completely retreated. By the shivering form she deduced that the hermaphrodite had been on the move for some time while she slept and was returning from its wanderings with the dead and the former residents of The Hi Brasil. She watched as it turned towards the bedroom. She gathered herself and followed with the slightest suspicion that Jack might actually be awake. Perhaps all this sleepwalking was a mind-game to test her love for him. And now she had erred by selfishly addressing those needs he was not fulfilling.

As she lay beside the cold form she felt an anger rise within her. She knew that the only thing that could heal the pain of his parents' death in these difficult days before their anniversary and beyond was her love. But he preferred to keep her at a distance using reason in the daytime while sending his spirit to walk with the dead at night. She firmly believed that the spirits that were now tampering with the house were those of Jack's parents. She'd never met them but she felt an antagonism towards them and wanted rid of them. Not least because their lingering ghosts had trapped him in that state in which she had imagined him, in the months of absence when she searched the city for him, only finding him in his chart. Latent, uncreative, his sun and moon extinguished.

Rosa had presumed her love would be enough to resuscitate him from that grief, but it hadn't and she had come to the conclusion that her love would never be enough if he didn't learn to love himself a little more and the world a little less.

IV
A Troublesome Corpse

According to the 7am news, the remains of Martin Meaney were stalled in London awaiting confirmation of their final journey. Rumours abounded that the British authorities would push for a quick interrment to avoid a focus for rising discontent in the Irish communities in Britain. Meaney's vocal advocacy of the innocence of the Birmingham Six, Guildford Four, not to mention the Maguires and Judith Ward had made him a figurehead for the disparate campaigns of recent years. Meaney was held in high esteem by immigrant communities in Britain. His 1966 literary memoir "We Are Born Astride The Gangway" was a staple of every first generation emigrant household.

The daily papers, Jack noticed, were full of his bravery at the side of the doomed fellow-poet Charlie Donnelly at the Battle of Jarama, while missing out on the key radicalising event of his life: Meaney's youthful apprenticeship at the side of Dixie Boran, the mastermind of the 1930s Castlecomer Soviet. For weeks Dixie Boran and his "communist anti-God cell" of coal-miners from across the Castlecomer Plateau had occupied the mines at Crettyard, Clogh, Deerpark and Skehana while above ground Priests, Proprietors and Police marshalled by the Fascist cop O'Duffy had blockaded the roads leading to the pit-heads. It fell to Martin Meaney, a skinny "hurrier" of coal, to climb the unofficial routes through the seams of anthracite and sandstone to seek out the sympathetic peasant providers of sustenance to the Soviet.

Jack was now concluding his obituary in the solitude of the Garden of Remembrance below their house. It would soon be typed up by Arlene and lain on the Poetry Collective's Gestetner for immediate publication as an insert to the Monthly Poetry Bulletin along with a call-to-all-poets to pitch for the Martin Meaney Memorial Medal. If the victory prize could not be engineered for the good of the collective, it might as well be thrown open to all-comers.

No report of Meaney's Soviet years – the Castlecomer Soviet that is - was to be found in any book. Perhaps because Meaney had not overtly addressed it in his 1966 "Gangway" memoir, which concentrated instead on the progressive times in the post-war building boom in Birmingham and London where the agile poet had plied his days on

38

Britain's high-rise project. Welder or fitter by day, poet by night, he had his finger on the pulse of the working man. While it appeared that Meaney had abandoned his native county, it was clear to Jack that this was far from the case. The landscape of his polite English world was in fact rent from that subterranean Kilkenny world of his youth: Grant's Flat, The Big Road, Catbrook, Darby's Run, Jarrow Seam were in fact part of the Castlecomer system, not to mention the seedy Gobbin Road, the spent corridor where a miner leaves his waste for the rats to take.

These were insights Jack had learned from retired and unemployed miners speaking in hushed tones and idling over long-drawn out pints of Smithwicks in the expanse of Castlecomer's Coalmine Lounge in the long and yawning summers of the mid-70s. Jack lived there with his mother in a house located, appropriately given the recent family separation, above the Coolbawn Fault. These miners tales were not solely about revolutionary promise but represented key insights into the interior and melancholic tone of Meaney's work.

Meaney was not known to visit 'Comer in those years. However, the landscapes of north Kilkenny were not kept at the margins of his writing as some would claim. He visited them every night. The experience of those weeks of pitched battles, the near starvation conditions and the final ascent to face O'Duffy's gloating mug and the wizened face of "lord and master" Capt R.H. Prior Wandesforde (who had sentimentally named one of the pits "Vera" after his delicate daughter) suffused Meaney's numerous collections. Castlecomer may have been the prelude to The Republican Congress which became the prelude to Spain but it was also the key to the interiority of the poet's work.

The Garden of Remembrance was stirring to life as Jack looked up from his note-book. He observed the splendour of the city's forgotten crucible: the jewel of the Hugh Lane with its myriad impressionists, the nicotine-tarred Dublin City Council Chambers where votes traded in grubby planning deals; the building behind the Chambers which housed Fowler's Orange Hall where a reputed dump of 60,000 Ulster Volunteers rifles could have swung the Rising if captured; to Cavendish Row where the revolution was executed. It was said, though Jack had never located it, that Collins had constructed a tunnel from Cassidy's under the Square to connect with the Sinn Féin offices; close by, the regal Rotunda where the same opportunist Collins had chosen life over death, success over failure by jumping the low fence that separated the condemned leaders from NCOs after the GPO.

The park attendants were hunting the bushes for the drunks and down and outs who made the park their home for the night. It was here Jack believed the Scaffolder had retired as night fell and where he now hoped to engage him in a conversation he believed he had walked away from the previous evening. There were better places to spend the night. The Hi Brasil for one. Nobody should be stuck for shelter, not least in the chill of March. As he stood and stretched he searched the faces of young and old alike as they too stepped out of their hypothermic and in some cases hypodermic slumber. The Scaffolder was not to be found among them.

It wasn't only for the good of the older man's health that Jack wanted to meet him again. He was curious as to why he had addressed Jack by telling him immediately of his profession. It was as if in that split second he knew who Jack was and therefore felt able to impart this significant part of his identity. If only Jack hadn't been in such a rush. He was convinced this man had something else to tell him.

Gazing along the façade of Parnell Square he could see that the curtains of the bedroom where he had left a soundly sleeping Rosa were now open. Time for breakfast. He had something to tell her, something just gleaned from the pages of this week's Bizniz satirical magazine. Their landlords, an elderly couple of Georgian enthusiasts, had been the subject of a hard-hitting article, which highlighted the multiplicity of their properties and their commitment to keeping them untenanted, bar the one tenant required by their insurance policy. Jack had made good of this folly by providing a home for the Poetry Collective. But he had gone as far as he could in using the available space without attracting the attention of the property management company. Otherwise he might have been able to accommodate Skiddy after his recent eviction.

Rosa didn't seem too interested. Instead she seemed taken with a subject he hadn't given much thought.
    - Jack, your Aunt Sarah phoned again yesterday about the anniversary mass.
    - Oh?
    - She was hoping you might read one of your poems.
Jack had not stepped foot inside the doors of a church since the double-funeral. He had not altered his opinion of the futility of such superstitious religious acts that were so bound up with the hegemony of the Catholic Church.

- Rosa, I might turn up for the meal afterwards.
- Think of it as a ceremonial ritual.
Here Rosa and he parted company.
- Look what the same ritualists did to Martin Meaney. Excommunication!
- You haven't been excommunicated.
No, but he wished he had. It might stop all these Legion of Mary types who stalked the Square, not to mention his God-fearing relatives trying to coax him back into the fold. Rosa seemed keen to continue the conversation, but he withdrew to a re-reading of the Bizniz article which worryingly highlighted "a particularly fine but semi abandoned premises on Parnell Square". The anonymous writer was obviously familiar with the history of the Hi Brasil.
- Jack?
This was more serious than it might have been.
- Jack, I think someone has been breaking into the house.
Jack put down the sarcastic rag.
- Why didn't you say?
- Someone left the front door open again last night.
Jack didn't like the poetry collective members having access to the building after hours and had only just recently changed the locks. Rosa was looking at him for a response. He couldn't think who it would be and sensed Rosa was up to her mumbo jumbo.
- The kitchen window leading to the fire escape was off the latch.
- Is anything missing?
- No!
She looked at him. He could see she was relieved he was taking her concerns seriously.
- It's more that things have been getting moved around.

The words "mumbo jumbo" teetered on the tip of his tongue when he remembered an incident before Rosa and he lived together. Tim and Jenny, a couple of junkies living at the top of the Square had been robbing all the houses on their side using the joined up roof-scape. Tim and Jenny liked to play mind games with their prey. In Jack's case they regaled him with a copy of Mein Kampf which got him going more than the invasion of his privacy or the loss of the cuff-links his mother had given him for his eighteenth birthday.
- I wonder if it could be Tim and Jenny?
Rosa seemed relieved that he was taking her fears of intrusion seriously.
- They did everyone on this side of the square, north of Granby Lane.

- You never told me!

- Because they were stopped.

- How?

- They broke into number 44. The Party didn't appreciate that.

- And?

- They received a visit from Community Concern and were told to stop or...

- Or?

- Or take a one-way trip to the Border.

- Well then it's hardly them.

- Maybe not. I'll ask around Rosa.

Rosa seemed unappeased by this, even though Jack felt like he was making a concession to her, well her paranoia. He hadn't heard a thing last night. In fact he hadn't slept so soundly for weeks. He was out of explanations and he needed to get down to Arlene who was typing and copying the obituary for him, but Rosa was now standing in his way. He could smell that familiar early morning scent of hers. The straps of her night dress fell loosely around her shoulders. Why was she looking so intently at him?

- You really have no idea who it could be, do you?

Rosa seemed to know more than she was letting on.

- Rosa, listen the magazine has to be in the shops.

He knew he was being economical with the truth, but didn't want to air his growing fears until he had proof.

- Jack, we need to talk.

- Rosa, please. The Bulletin...

- ...is very urgent I know. What about this evening?

- We're having that Policy and Procedures meeting.

He saw how upset she became at the mention of this meeting. It really was like walking on egg-shells with her this morning. Maybe she wanted to be there. But what was the point? She was only a probationary member and therefore had no vote. Asking her to be there was only pandering to her sensitivities about Kate Keane and as there was nothing going on between him and Kate Keane, nothing whatsoever, he didn't see why he should suggest she be there. He grabbed his jacket and saw how disappointed she was, but he needed to leave. He was almost out the door when she pulled him back.

- By the way Jack, did you find your pyjamas this morning?

It was only then that he remembered waking up completely naked, his pyjamas nowhere to be seen.

- What about my pyjamas?

- They were lying on the stairs two floors down when I woke earlier.

42

- I see.

He realised he said this like this was the most ordinary thing in the world. He felt himself laughing. Rosa was not amused.

- Have you any idea how they got there Jack?
- Should I?

For a moment, Jack thought Rosa was going to tell him something important, but she suddenly seemed to deflate at the confrontational tone in his voice. She drew her dressing gown around her shoulders in a sudden show of modesty. He was confused by her behaviour but he needed to get out of there. His worst fears were beginning to dawn. This had all the marks of Tim and Jenny's mind games.

- Rosa, I've got to go.

He should really have stayed to see what was wrong with her. Perhaps he should have invited her to the committee meeting. Then she would have felt patronised. Sometimes you just couldn't placate Rosa.

While Arlene inserted the obituary into the Bulletins in her deliberate almost trance like way he ambled up the Square to No. 44. Seamus, the security man and a Long Kesh veteran with a tattooed figure of Hibernia on his right arm, was sweeping the front step while surveying the street for would-be Loyalist attackers. He barely acknowledged Jack as he glowered at the perennial unmarked car parked across the road by the Rotunda Outpatients. The expression did not soften as the ex-prisoner's eyes came to rest on the inconsequential Jack. Number 44 was in mourning after the gunning down in cold blood of three of their colleagues in Gibraltar the previous week.

- How's about you comrade?
- Tá mé go maith a chara. Is tú fhéin?
- Go maith, go maith. What can I do for you?

This was the extent of both their Irish so Jack got down to business.

- I have some post in the house for Tim and Jenny. Have you seen them about?

Seamus looked at him suspiciously.

- Have you checked it, comrade?

Jack shook his head.

- Burn it!
- I can't do that, a chara.
- Postmark?

He thought of the package he had indeed received for Tim and Jenny some months before which he had dutifully delivered around to them.

- Amsterdam.
- Burn it. That's where they are. No one writes to those wasters but themselves.

43

        - But why can't I just drop it into them?
He needed to know where they were.
            - It'll have to wait.
            - It will?
            - They're in Amsterdam. It's always Amsterdam.

He was torn between relief at being able to dismiss Tim and Jenny as likely intruders and horror at their use of him in their drug distribution activities. The thought of the contents of that package wending its way through the veins of Tim and Jenny's desperate clientele made him sick to the pit of his stomach.

As he cycled up Belvedere Place into Gardiner Place he looked up at the spire of Saint George's, clad in its perennial cloak of scaffold. He imagined his scaffolder holed up in his nest, in a place no ordinary mortal could reach. He realised his body was covered in a cold sweat. All he could think of was the tape, the tape bearing the reflections of his former pupil Terry Crowe which he had so diligently transcribed the previous night and was today planning to deliver to Mountjoy after his Bulletin run. It occurred to him that even though Terry had delivered the tape through his boy-courier, that Terry might have graduated to the sunnier side of Mountjoy's walls. Was the tape in fact a calling card from a recently liberated Terry? Had the same Terry broken into the Hi Brasil and stolen Jack's pyjamas as some prank? If Tim and Jenny were out of their heads in Amsterdam planning their next importation who else could it be?

He needed to know for himself if Terry was at liberty. He set a course northwards and within five minutes he was dismounting his bike outside Mountjoy. At the entrance to the Training Unit he told the screw on duty that he had a delivery for one of their inmates.
            - He says you gave up on him.
The screw related.
            - He said that?
The screw volunteered a sly smile. They all knew that Terry had given Jack the door over Jack's excessive consciousness-raising teaching techniques and when Jack tried to convince Terry he was oppressed, Terry flipped the lid and said that there was fuck all wrong with his mind.

Jack found himself eyeballing the screw, pretending not to recall his miserable visage from his last visit. He had a thing about people in

44

uniforms who profited from carrying out the state's dirty business. It never occurred to him that someone had to perform this joyless task. It did occur to him suddenly that if Terry was there the screws would read the transcription of Terry's thoughts (which included some fairly seditious things about the prison regime) and Terry would be punished.

- He's not here!

Perhaps Terry had been moved to Portlaoise to tame his anarchic spirit. He felt guilty at wishing this were the case, but the prospect of Terry being at liberty presented him with a problem he could do without.

- Well where is he then?

- Probably up to his balls in his missus or up a drain pipe in Blackrock.

- Out?!

The screw could not have missed the alarm in Jack's voice.

- I'm afraid so. Now he's your problem, not ours.

Jack was still in shock as he wheeled his bike back onto the truck rattled North Circular Road. Terry Crowe was out and was for some reason trying to enter Jack's world, at the very time that world was coming apart. But why break into his house? What was wrong with the door-bell or the telephone? If Terry was trying to reconnect as yesterday's tape delivery suggested, it was probably him breaking into The Hi Brasil while he and Rosa slept. Until he knew otherwise he needed to be more sensitive to Rosa's fears of psychic disturbance.

How would he react when he finally came face to face with Scary Terry Crowe? So much had happened in Terry's absence from the Poetry Collective. The Poetry Bulletin had been launched. Its viability was in the balance. Jack's parents had died in unforeseen circumstances. Rosa had come to live with him. The Soviet Union was on its last legs. A more advanced stage of communism awaited its collapse.

V
The DD In Skiddy

It could have been the smell of detergent from the jakes still clinging to the bar-man's hands as he handed Skiddy his first pint of the day, but it was not going down well. Perhaps it was the cigarette breath of his drinking partner, lounge lizard and editor of Bizniz magazine Donal Dolan. Or maybe it was the sweetly-sick fizz from Donal's large bottle of Double Diamond ale being poured in jitters.

Skiddy had been snared by his drinking partner as he reeled out the door of The Long Hall the night before and summoned for duty as drinking buddy for the morning recovery. With dole day distant, there was only one thing for it. He had already prostituted himself to this lizard, so why stay away? One good reason. He had a poem to write. If he had only seized the advantage after his court with Jenkins the night before he would still have money in his pocket and a draft for the competition.

However, his stock was high with DD Dolan since his penning of the piece on the Ceaucescus of Georgiana and their crime of leaving their vast properties all but tenantless, oblivious to the chronic housing lists and rack rented flat-dwellers like Skiddy. DD appeared to have enjoyed the representations made to Bizniz on behalf of the Overends by their agents Hanley and Slaughter. They were keen, he said, to ascertain which of the care-takers of their ninety properties might be the source of the information.
     - Conscienceless Charlatans masquerading as Quaint Conservationists, don't you know.
Skiddy didn't give a tuppenny if they found out. He had only written the article to get back at Jack for not letting him take a free room in the hotel after his eviction for non-payment from that flea pit in Rathmines. He wasn't sure how long he would last in the digs his mother had arranged for him in nearby Ranelagh. The landlady was already tut-tutting.

Donal Dolan punctuated every sentence with "don't you know", a quaint Dublin tic that Skiddy found infuriating, but which assisted the current user in overcoming a minor stutter. Skiddy awaited elucidation from his media mentor, but it didn't come, so he went to the jakes while DD settled himself.

As he relieved himself Skiddy regretted the brace of pints downed in last night's race to closing time. The poem he had been mulling over the night before – a tale of unrequited love for a woman in the thrall of a rival - now had the smell of stale lust about it. "When the Angel woos the clay/He'd lose his wings at the dawn of the day". He would have to rekindle its more ethereal promise and desist from lusting until he had the poem in the bag. The sound of lively chat emanating from the bar suggested that DD's next meeting would take place there. This is how he offered his writers anonymity, migrating from lounge to bar, from bar to lounge, like some hot-shot hospital consultant or priest.

Skiddy examined his media mentor as he padded across the lounge on the new Clarkes brogues his mother had sent him from Galway. DD was shaking like some auld one in a home for the bewildered, the kind barman and the ambient lounge the one polite thing in this man's routine which revolved around dirt-digging and a daily dose of Double-Diamond.

Concern for DD's well-being was pushed aside as he remembered he was there to do business. The problem about getting paid or subbed by Bizniz magazine was that they only paid by cheque. Because they were always being busted by libel actions these cheques regularly bounced and the only establishment that would honour them was Cluxton's Lounge. A kind of symbiosis prevailed between Bizniz and Cluxton's. As DD spent most of his time working out of here you would never get away without a brace of pints under your belt. DD practised a form of mentor tax.

DD was discussing last night's football match with Lorcan Cluxton and musing on the team's chances in the forthcoming "Euros". Skiddy hadn't fancied DD as a football man but football frenzy was taking its hold on the headlines. What a bore. Bread and circuses for the masses. Would they ever get down to brass tacks? Another death-rattling cough from DD made him feel he was indeed in the home for the bewildered, departure depot. However, once cleared, it proved to be DD's call to business.
- Anything for me this week?
The request came like music to Skiddy's ears. He decided to tell him about Paddy Jenkins' visit to the poetry collective. DD seemed interested.
- Bloody chancer, don't you know!
No I don't know. Elucidate. DD was obviously aware of Paddy Jenkins.

A smile crossed his weak mouth and crumpled chin which Skiddy noticed he hid behind a thin mess of Desperate Dan stubble. The life of a media reptile. Was this to be Skiddy's destiny? His true vocation.
- Shoot.

Skiddy gave DD a run down on his encounter with Paddy Jenkins and what he had subsequently gleaned in his trawl of the city's drinking dens the previous night. He could see DD mentally ticking boxes as Skiddy aired his theory about Jenkins' frustrations with the Sam Beckett biography and the reasons for his courtship of Meaney prior to his death. It looked like Jenkins had been preparing for the eventuality of Meaney's death for some time. An Honorary PhD had been awarded two years previously in return for which Meaney promised his papers to the college. Skiddy's suspicions of Jenkins' plans for a Meaney Industry were not far off the mark if the broadening smile on DD's lips was to be believed. He barrelled on: this vast endeavour he ventured might in time include a symposium to launch Martin Meaney to the world as part of the annual Cúirt Festival in Galway; Bank of Eire's sponsorship of an annual Meaney award as part of their new kulturally kind kapitalist image; The cognoscenti to buy into Meaney's elevation by agreeing to contribute to the forthcoming Festschrift proclaiming the dead revolutionary man of letters, not to mention the summer school in desolate North Kilkenny. Once the jig-saw was in place Jenkins would have little difficulty convincing his London publishers to commission one of Paddy's popular biographies of the talented and the dead.
- Poor M-Meaney.
A tear appeared in Donal Dolan's left eye. Oh Jesus. He forgot that Donal Dolan had been in one of these lefty revolutionary sects, though you'd never have thought it from the reactionary guff that be-decked Bizniz magazine. Peddlars of cynicism and character assassination, material Skiddy enjoyed but which was more likely to induce resignation in the masses than revolt.
- Poor fucker is right. He is about to be placed on the butcher's block of acadaemia.
Skiddy surmised.
- I could tell you a thing or two, don't you know...
DD stalled in mid-sentence. Skiddy realised that his metre had run out and signalled to the barman for replenishment.
- He won't get away with it.
- Why?
Skiddy disliked his thesis being challenged.

- Because we won't let him.

He looked Skiddy in the eye.

- I want him taken down.
- He's a smooth operator, Donal.
- But he's vain. He has no real interest in Meaney.
- Can you blame him? He's trying to make a silk purse…

DD nearly choked on the frothy dregs of his pint but recovered his swallow with a sideways glance at Skiddy that left him in no uncertain terms of his dismissal of this statement. The delivery of a pair of large bottles softened his wheeze.

- Martin Meaney was no maker of sow's ears.

Skiddy needed to kick, if only to be taken off the case. Shafting Paddy Jenkins might be attractive in other circumstances but he had his poetic ambitions to think about. He could seize the Meaney Medal and Money as long as he maintained his anonymity. With Hanley and Slaughter Property Management on the warpath his anonymity was far from safe.

- No one, but a bunch of old lefties can be bothered with Meaney. He is not a poet of any standing.

Donal Dolan, who had once been a leftie of principal let the comment pass. He had larger fish to fry.

- Well, someone else is in the frame.
- Who?

Donal shook his head..

- Jenkins has made enemies over the years.
- Clearly.

Skiddy looked cheekily at his mentor. Resentment for their subject had soured the older man's face. Under Skiddy's examination DD copped himself on and stared back at Skiddy. They were approaching the end of their round, but Donal Dolan showed little sign of calling for more: a new engagement awaited him in the bar. Just as well. Skiddy already felt pissed as he straightened himself in his seat. He needed to collect his cheque and get the fuck out of here. Donal Dolan eye-balled him.

- Someone is writing the definitive Life of Meaney.
- Who?
- If I knew I wouldn't be offering you good money to find out.

He said tetchily, then tried to calm himself.

- All I know is that it's a serious piece of biography.
- And Jenkins is trying to steal a march?

DD nodded.

- He wants to deliver the funeral oration to gain credibility for the rush-job he's planning to write from the Meaney Papers that of course he and only he has his hands on.

49

Skiddy desisted from rubbing his hands together at the hint of a bitter feud, and the prospect of profiting from it. Would that his vying with Jack might someday elevate to this epic level. The right feud could be the making of a reputation. He watched as Donal Dolan rummaged around in his back pocket for the cheque book. There it was in a mass of bookies' dockets and unpaid parking fines.

For now he needed to concentrate on short term goals. Money. If he couldn't throw a few bob together how else was he to court Rosa? With Comrade Jack consumed with saving the world, now was Skiddy's chance. However, Skiddy was convinced that Jack also presented the major barrier to his winning of the Martin Meaney Memorial Medal. Despite his all-for-one nonsense, he reckoned Jack would try to seize it behind everyone's back. He would have to be taken out for this reason alone.

His heart sank as DD slipped the cheque-book back into his pocket having found the piece of paper he was looking for. Christ he was prepared to squeeze his balls to get this story. This was not in the plan. Donal sensed his disappointment.
        - Call yourself a judge of d-decent poetry?
Donal Dolan glared at him.
        - Martin Meaney was no sow's ear.
        - OK, OK. I'm out of here.
        - You're a fucker!
Lorcan Cluxton gazed from behind the bar where he was methodically drying glasses and smiled knowingly at the roasting of the cub. DD took note and dropped his voice but not the intensity.
        - Fucker.
The message was no less severe. You're a maniac thought Skiddy, a dipsofuckingmaniac, and quickly backed off.

As he re-entered the Spring morning he recoiled at the chill in the air. There was a brightness to the day he always associated with this time of year, a brightness he could do without. Coiscéim Coiligh his granny in Conamara called these days. The step of a cock in the daily angling of the sun. He could do without the sun. These days, he longed for the nights. Daytime reminded him of what an idle bastard he was becoming. He was a reptile after all and he needed the shadow of the night. He had hoped the Daily Dose with Dirt Digging Donal Double Diamond Desperate Dan Don't You Know Dolan in the Departure Depot would settle his hangover. But he had over-reached, in more ways than one. Ideally his relating of Jenkins' manipulative ways was a story that should hit the press when Skiddy had the Meaney Medal safely in his mitt. But Bizniz already appeared to have Paddy Jenkins in their sights for a proper "doing".

He could walk away from the story to concentrate on the poem, but how else was he to pursue Rosa if he didn't have cash from Bizniz? She was so wasted on Jack he wondered if the fucker even noticed the dame anymore. There was something strange about their relationship, something distinctly a-sexual. He wondered if it was one of these platonic relationships that people got themselves wrapped up in to escape the real cut and thrust of romantic love. Under that prim tight arsed exterior, she had it in her. When he thought of her, he thought of poetry. Poetry. But in going to these lengths to woo her was he being set off the path of creativity? "When the angel woos the clay..." Should he not be doing right by the poem for the competition and stall the enquiry for DD, channel his thoughts of lust and admiration for Rosa into an award-winning poem and then claim the dame? Fuck it, it was too good an opportunity to miss. There was no poetry without Rosa, but there would be no courtship without cash.

VI
The Serpent Smiles

Rosa reached up and removed the Great Book from the reference section of the Alchemist's Head. Leafing through the Opus Magnum, she came to the revelatory passage and read it aloud in preparation for tonight's ceremony. "First we bring together, then we putrefy, we break down what has been putrefied, we purify the divided, we unite the purified and harden it. In this way is One made from man and woman." (Buchlein vom Stein der Weisen)

She deduced from these wise words that what needed to be brought together in the ceremony she had planned for tonight was Jack's dead parents; the process of their putrefaction to be completed; their divided selves to be purified (not putrefied) and then united. In order for Rosa and Jack to be united, to be as One, she believed that Jack had to know that his parents were truly at peace.

Rosa knew that Jack not only remained troubled by their sudden deaths - even if he wouldn't admit it - but also by their state of disunity at the time of their deaths. It was widely believed that they had crashed into the canal having missed all warning signs on the road while having a blazing row. Witnesses from a nearby restaurant where they had been dining had apparently testified to their disagreement at the inquest.

Despite Jack's belief in togetherness, Rosa knew that he had experienced a dysfunctional upbringing characterised by a state of marital warfare. Rosa presumed that the Poetry Collective represented a kind of family, which he was trying to make function in the way his own hadn't. If he persisted with this hope he was destined to repeat the disappointment. His attempts to place some kind of order on The Poetry Collective would prove similarly unsuccessful. Could he not see that they were an eclectic bunch of individuals who had nothing else in common other than their need of light and heat and perhaps the resolution of their own dysfunctional family backgrounds which they too should be attempting to resolve by other means, be it poetry or therapy?

Rosa believed that if Jack was in search of a surrogate family he should be seeking that with her. However, this was not going to happen until he was faced with the unspoken pain about his own family. If what he sought in his sleepwalking was a re-unification with his parents for a proper farewell, then she felt it her duty to assist. For the process of putrefaction to be commenced she needed to have Jack seated with her in the energy circle which she would create with the family relics that littered their rooms in the Hi Brasil. She would then commence a séance in which she and Jack would commune with his parents. He would never do this while awake so her only hope was to do it while way-laid on his now familiar pattern of sleep-walking. She was under no illusion that the process of putrefaction prescribed by The Great Work would require more than one session. However, it was urgent the process commence.

On arrival at the shop this morning, Rosa had checked his chart as she was wont to do on a regular, in fact, daily basis. She became alarmed by the rapid ascent of Mercury. An impending journey. This journey would not be without its perils. It puzzled her because it seemed inconsistent with his current preoccupation with events local and the more cyclical nature of his activities which she had been carefully mapping. This mooted journey would involve water. This spoke to her of danger, perhaps an attempt to repeat his parents' fatal actions as was often the pattern with an unacknowledged trauma.

Rosa had been so engrossed in Jack's chart and the study of The Great Work that she had barely noticed the shop door open and a man in his early thirties enter. She took enough heed of him to notice that he wasn't one of their regular customers. His cropped haircut, trim denim jacket and drain-pipe jeans seemed ill-fitting and oddly out of fashion. She would never say this in Jack's presence but he was of the underclass, so to speak, the kind of man more likely to frequent the bookies or the dole office than a shop specialising in The Occult. However, she noticed the tattoos: a predictable fire-breathing dragon on one arm and a cherub on the other. She could not make out the tattoo on his neck, but thought she saw the head of a bird, a raven or a crow perhaps, peering out above the neck-line of his T-shirt.

It was not unusual for people to rob from the shop. They stocked some rare books such as The Great Work and while this man might not be planning to rob for himself he might be robbing to order. What also alarmed her was that although he seemed to be concentrating on the book he had removed from the shelves, the book was in fact upside down. If he was unable to read, as this suggested, could he really be intending to rob it, to order or otherwise? The air was so heavy she decided to pierce it.

- Is there anything I can help you with?

Terry Crowe remained staring at the book as if not having heard what she said, casually turning the page to indicate his preoccupation with the book. She went back to her reading while keeping a watchful eye. Suddenly out of the blue.

- I'm looking for books on body art, tattoos.
Would you know much about that, dear?

So he did have a purpose. Rosa was relieved.

- I'm afraid not. There are places that specialise in that.
- So what do you do here?
- We're a shop dedicated to The Occult.

Rosa did her best to maintain a calm voice in the face of the man's heavy vibration.

- Is that the devil's business?
- The devil doesn't exist.
- You must be fucking joking?

She was not expecting this aggression. However Rosa was tired of The Occult being interpreted as mere superstition.

- Can you prove otherwise?

The man fell into silence, casually turning his book the right way up. She thought he might be upset by her discounting of the devil.

- You're welcome to look at any of the images we have if you're planning another tattoo.

He neither seemed to acknowledge or ignore her, flicking over some more pages. Shortly after, he left. He left behind an uncomfortable feeling in the shop. When she went down to rearrange the shelves, she realised that the book he had been reading was gone. He had obviously taken her offer of help a little too literally.

The shop remained quiet. After all, many of their regulars were dispersed to the various ancient sites away from the capital for the Spring Equinox, to Sliabh na Cailleach in County Meath or Carrowkeel in County Sligo. So she read on: "the king in the sea swims and cries with a loud voice: whoever catches and rescues me, to him I will give a great reward" (M Maier, Atalanta Fugiens, Oppenheim, 1618). How far would she allow Jack venture into danger before saving him, so that he would know that despite his kingly virtues he could not exist in complete autonomy. Presuming someone else didn't rescue him.

Rosa had earlier decided not to attend the Poetry Collective for the debate on Policy and Procedures, not least because she did not agree with Jack's insistence that bursaries and awards secured by members be shared amongst victor and vanquished alike. The talented, among whom she did not number herself, should be rewarded. There was a natural order to the movement of the heavens which should be heeded. To deny this was to promote imbalance and disorder. However, there was another interpretation to the appearance of water in Jack's chart. The Aquarian Kate Keane had become a regular presence in their lives. Because she lived out of town she would sometimes stay in one of the many unoccupied rooms in The Hi Brasil. She was reliable and knew the score. It was on one of these evenings that Rosa had offered to do her chart. She could hardly say that she knew her though when Rosa mentioned her visit to Sliabh na Cailleach, Kate described with enthusiasm her regular visits there. Other than that she said very little about herself or where she came from. Rosa found her unnecessarily secretive. Perhaps what irked her most was that Kate had known Jack longer than she had known him. She felt it was this that lay at the heart of Kate's secretiveness. If Kate was the reason for the appearance of water in Jack's chart, she could not allow it to progress without early intervention. She must go to the meeting. Kate had to be stopped.

Skiddy had obviously been busy rallying his forces for the inevitable vote. Some of the Poetry Collective's least active and obscure voting members had turned up for the spat. How Skiddy had cajoled them into turning up she was unsure. These were people who barely made it out of bed before nightfall most evenings, before taking up residence in Grogan's Bar on Castle Street or the The Long Hall. Bar-stool poets and artists. Dublin was full of them. No one liked to describe themselves as unemployed. So much easier to describe yourself as what you thought you should be, the assignation without the qualification. Jack had already had the floor as she entered and Skiddy, now set on his predictable but passionately delivered case for unfettered competition. By the nods of the assembled mob, it was clear that Skiddy, charismatic and articulate, would win the day.

As his eyes darted backwards and forwards to his listeners that image that had been playing at Rosa's imagination for some time was now beginning to crystallise for her. For weeks a symbol had been swimming around in her consciousness that she knew was connected to Skiddy's attentions towards her. It was only then that it was beginning to form for her.

Clearly quick-witted and someone of talent he was a contradictory character, always restless and turning back on himself, always teasing and craving an audience, darting here and there looking for an opening in a person's defences. He certainly had the character for the cut and thrust of poetry. As he spoke, she felt his foot edge up her shin. Had he sensed her idle attention to him. Taken by surprise she was slow to react. As it shifted about, the image suddenly became clear to her. Closing her eyes, the image of a serpent appeared to her. She found herself smiling at the realisation. Opening her eyes she realised the smile was a source of encouragement for him as his foot moved further up her shin. How devious a character he was to be trying to simultaneously reduce Jack and seduce her. Rosa crossed her legs and managed to successfully expel the intruder, but not quickly enough to deter him from further mischief-making.

With only Kate Keane to back him up, Jack's appeals for poets to stick together in order to overcome their collective financial difficulties had fallen on deaf ears. Kate carried some weight with these status-conscious poets if only because of her early involvement in the Collective. She appealed to the assembled poets to emulate the spirit of some putative earlier generation of poets who had allowed personal profit play second fiddle to the good of the country. She argued that the Poetry Collective should be wary of Jenkins' ability to deliver on his promises. She saw how Jack looked at Kate admiringly upon this suggestion which hurt even more for it was she who had told Professor Jenkins about the existence of the Poetry Collective in the first place, placing him on the mailing list for the Monthy Poetry Bulletin. The appearance of water in Jack's chart that day was beginning to make sense. The Aquarian Kate Keane was making up to Jack. However, Rosa still wasn't going to confront her. She left that to Skiddy
        - Why so suspicious? The guy is giving us a chance to raise our profiles. Isn't that right Rosa?
Skiddy's question took her by surprise.
        - As a non-voting member I don't have a say in this.
        - Surely you have an opinion? Can he deliver?
Rosa, as Jack knew, was never one to suppress an opinion. Not to answer would have been answer enough for him. She felt in not answering she would not be true to herself. If Jack had really wanted to win this point of principal he should have threatened the lot of them with eviction. After all they were only here because of the risks he was taking with the tenancy. It was too late for that.
        - I don't have any reason to believe he won't.

Rosa saw Jack's face drop at her intervention. Skiddy's face broke into a smile.

    - Q.E.D!

Arlene whispered to one of their number for translation, while a rueful Jack translated.

    - Quod Erat Demonstrandum

Rosa awoke at the kitchen table. There was a stiff breeze blowing from somewhere. The candles she had lit in the hall-way to create the energy circle for Jack to enter when the inevitable sleepwalking commenced had been extinguished. She rushed into the hallway to check if the hall door was open, but the bolt which she had secured earlier was still in place. She climbed the stairs to the bedroom and saw that Jack had vacated the space, his tether untied.

Rushing back into the landing she realised the source of the breeze. A ladder had been placed in the centre of the energy circle she had created of candles and family relics. That ladder led to the sky-light and the heavens beyond. Fearing the worst she climbed out onto the roof where a stiff southerly filled her light night clothes. There was no sign of Jack. A quick look over the edge revealed he hadn't fallen. She was about to descend into the house when she saw a figure move in the darkness. A hooded man stood watching her. Catching the gaze of his sparkling eyes she observed how the man revealed the palms of his hands to ease her terror while backing away from her with great agility along the parapet wall, oblivious to the great heights. He didn't fit the description of the junky raiders Jack had told her about, but he did seem to know his way around the perilous roof-scape.

    - What do you want?

The man who had the appearance of a building worker raised the palms of his large hands again, gave no answer other than to beckon her. She ventured around the tall red-bricked chimney stack and there perched four stories above the street she found Jack standing on the parapet wall of the neighbouring house, naked. The intruder stood close by as if in careful attendance, whispering gently in Jack's ear. Jack appeared not to respond, but then gazed skywards while walking blindly along the parapet.

    - No!

Rosa attempted to alert him. The intruder immediately raised his hands in assurance, wanting Rosa to step up to the parapet beside him, which she did, placing a vice-like grip on Jack's arm before steering him away from the edge. When she turned to address the man he was swinging from the lightning rod. All of a sudden he dropped to an iron balcony below before scaling to the street with the assistance of a drain-pipe. Rosa laid her two hands on Jack's shoulder and breathed of the night air. By the time she looked over the edge the building worker or whatever he was had effected a spider-man like descent and had disappeared possibly into the darkness of the basement.

Getting Jack back down the ladder without waking him was difficult enough and Rosa decided not to proceed with the planned séance. The energy circle had worked to the extent that having entered it the only way out for the sleepwalking Jack had been up, perhaps through the intercession of the intruder aiding his ascent. She realised that her lack of thoroughness in her task had nearly had disastrous results. She needed to find some other solution to Jack's extreme loss, before he embarked on the journey she had predicted for him.

It occurred to her as she lay with him in her arms that in the two years they had been together, he had never told her he loved her. It wasn't just his shyness with the first person singular. It was his distance in relating to the other. It was as if for most of the time she didn't exist for him. The thought filled her with a sudden terror. She needed to hear those words: Rosa, I love you. Until now she had presumed it, but of late she had begun to wonder. Was there something going on with Kate Keane? She needed to know what he felt for her, not least because their relationship was under threat. The uninvited attention from Skiddy had provided its own pressures.

Rosa felt Jack stir and drew him closer to her sensing his spirit arriving back to join his body from wherever it had been, perhaps out along the canal in search of his parents. The warmth was coming back into his body and between his legs his sex was emerging. She thought now might be the time to bring him back into this life and possess him once again, but as if sensing her desire he pulled away from her. Don't turn away from me like that hermaphrodite. Would he never satisfy her again? Was this why the serpent had been sent? To satisfy this need in her?

She had to admit that the sensation of Skiddy caressing the inside of her leg had given her some pleasure, so while she climbed on top of the sleeping Jack and held his limp sex against hers she could not prevent the snake from circling the bed. It slithered along her back in a swift motion and coiled itself around her neck in a rough action that made her throw her head back exposing her to its poisonous kisses. She was suffocating with the sensation as it caressed her breasts, its scaly skin igniting nerve ends she didn't realise she had.

Meanwhile, Jack was growing hard in her hands and she began to rock against him. Yes, finally they were together even if he was unaware of it. For a moment it was only she and he, the snake retreating jealously to its corner the harder Jack grew. Just like that first time, but better. Would he ever tell her that he loved her? Tell me Jack tell me. She couldn't ever hear those words. She could never hear him saying those words. The snake rallied again, coiling around her mid-riff trying to drag her away for himself. It slid down her sweaty arse. Yes, that was it. He would never touch her there. That's not what it was made for he said. Yes it was said the snake and he was right. Tell me Jack. Just tell me and I'll send the snake away. Too late. The snake had her in its power. The sensation was starting in her feet and beginning to move up through her body, lifting her. A bright light shone above her in the dark. Now, it was just Rosa alone in the night. Free of space and time, climbing and climbing into that light lost in space and time, until gradually the orgasm began to ebb and she slumped down beside him in the bed.

Finally, Rosa could sleep.

So, now I have them on the move. My band of poxy poets. Primed, promising and unpredictable. Unsettled in their boxes. Let's say that so far I have been stirring the pot gently. I have been sowing conflict. This all-for-one idea is not of interest to me. Without competition there is no uncertainty. Without uncertainty, no drama, no creative edge.

There is still plenty of time for any of them to seize the prize. In that time I must be sure to plunder them for their best, squeeze them dry of their miserable-ness. The forging of the sayable from the unmentionable is not a pretty business.

A pauper's business.

For now, let me revel in the freedom of the city in its millennium year. My absence and the distance of time has given me a taste for its streets again. Believe me, it is not all doom and gloom. There are the signs of promise even if for most of these years it has been a case of rats fleeing a sinking ship. The people, my people are dreaming of higher things. Poetry still has its place.

Time to apply some pressure. I am feeling hungry for results. I want to see the pain. There is a prize at the end of the pain. Each-way bets are off. Love has been pushed aside and lust is pushing to the fore.

I don't mind giving one thing away. One of my Trinity will take the prize.

VII
Ghost Writer

- Remember me? I'm the one who told you to climb. Have you forgotten about me already?

- What do you want from me?!

- I am a scaffolder. Foresake these walls. Foresake the ground.

- But how can I?

Just let go and you'll see.

- Don't look back, don't look down, keep your feet off the ground.

Jack's eyes flicked open. Dazed, he looked around him to see who it was had been speaking with him. No one appeared to be paying him any heed. Good. He had managed to nod off in the middle of the busy Poetry Collective office. If someone hadn't been talking to him, he might have been talking to himself. His mouth was dry. He had obviously been snoozing for some time. What a vivid dream. Floating above Parnell Square, the fine houses, the ballrooms, the Rotunda, Fowler's Orange Hall, the cruciform shape of the Garden of Remembrance.

This was happening to him of late. He had dreamed nights ago of making love to Rosa. When he woke in the morning he found the signs of lovemaking and realised that it hadn't been a dream. However, he had remembered nothing of the circumstances of their coupling. But this voice in his head was so vivid. It was the voice of the scaffolder who he hadn't seen in nearly a week, but who had found his place in his dreams. How had he got from there to here? Had he imagined him in the first place? This confusion, this loss of control unsettled him. He took out his notebook and made a note: "The Scaffolder Calls. Flying above Parnell Square."

Jack observed the bustling room about him. The Poetry Collective office was busy. News of the Martin Meaney Memorial Medal carried in the Poetry Bulletin had swelled their ranks. Poets had materialised from all over the city to collect an entry form and to get details of the prize and closing dates. There had been complaints about the imminent deadline. Jack and Arlene had done their best to explain that the call for submissions had been occasioned by the death of Martin Meaney and no one but a visionary could have foretold this event.

Arlene had been dealing efficiently with the complaints as she merely repeated the script that Professor Jenkins had provided: "From Haiku to Epic Form, the English language is the norm, Close of business March Twenty Four". The Poetry Collective had come of age. What a shame it was about to end.

He looked down at the letter received that morning and re-read it just to confirm for himself the contents. "Dear Mister Lennon, As part of a routine review of our property portfolio, we request your presence at our offices this coming Friday…" Why so formal? The role of care-taker had come about through an old school friend Johnny Slaughter Jnr. who knowing Jack perennially short of money and unaverse to the rough and tumble of Dublin 1 had installed him in Parnell Square, under certain conditions, as caretaker of the former Hi Brasil Hotel. He had no formal agreement and no security of tenure. What had unsettled that mutually beneficial relationship? Rent free for him and an insurable property for his landlords and their agents Hanley and Slaughter.

He wanted to unburden himself of this news to somebody. He looked around the room, which had become a hub of activity in recent days. Had Hanley and Slaughter got wind of the heavy traffic of visitors to their Parnell Square property? He recognised poets who had not crossed the threshold before, unsure about their poetry or the value of collective creative action perhaps, now chattering enthusiastically while waiting to collect their entry forms. They had Professor Jenkins to thank for this. More accurately, they had Meaney to thank. Arlene was politely if firmly repeating the guidelines and reminding the anxious poets of the solemnity of the enterprise: a commemorative poem for Martin Meaney.

Still there were further complaints about the shortness of time before the closing date and accusations of an inside track for a select few members of the Collective. He couldn't be bothered to explain once again that the memorial medal had only come to pass because of Meaney's death some few days ago. Given the delay in getting Meaney's body to Holyhead and forecasts of rough seas causing a backlog on the channel crossings, yes there might be some leeway of hours with the deadline but the winning poem would have to be selected in time for presentation at the secular memorial service now scheduled for Trinity Church in three days time.

Jack wondered what Meaney would have made of all this fuss and tension. He probably would have enjoyed it. After all, Meaney had been a driving force behind the London Poetry Collective which had formed in 1967 around a band of revolutionary-minded poets frequenting Soho's French House bar. This was around the time he had teamed up with west of Ireland poet Uinsionn OFlatharta and together the pair had motivated the London Poetry Collective to take on the cause of Civil Rights in Northern Ireland. Together they had manned the barricades of Derry's Bogside and had taken on the might of the British Army with words for bullets. It was these tales of derring do that made Jack feel like he was born in the wrong time. He was sick of this every-man-for himself decade, epitomised by the signatory of this letter, the pompous little yuppy Johnny Slaughter Jnr., heir to at least half of the Hanley and Slaughter property portfolio. What would Meaney have done in the face of such pomposity? An occupation of the building was in his thoughts, but could he count on the solidarity of the collective membership. The recent vote made him doubt it. He needed to speak with someone.

At one end of the room Kate Keane was methodically pushing copies of The Poetry Bulletin into envelopes, having helpfully agreed to deal with all postal subscriptions. At the other side of the room, huddled up against the radiator Skiddy was writing intensely, pausing periodically to fart or pick his nose. As if sensing Jack's gaze, he stopped writing and scanned the assembly of chattering poets with contempt.
  - Do you fucking mind?
The poets went quiet. Skiddy dropped his voice.
  - I am creating.
Arlene looked at him disapprovingly, her confidence buoyed by her new role as information officer.
  - Stephen Kieran, I'm trying to take care of the public.
Skiddy looked at Arlene, then at the woman to whom Arlene was attending, now in possession of the entry form.
  - I wouldn't bother if I were you.
Having got everyone's attention again, he mumbled something underneath his breath, something like:
  - They've already made up their minds about the winner.
Silence descended on the room as the prospective poets exchanged nervous glances with each other, then at the forms for which they had probably spent precious bus fare money to come and collect. Most of them were canny enough to deduce from Skiddy's continued writing that the game was far from up and returned to their chattering. Jack

looked again at the letter from Hanley and Slaughter. A doubt lingered. Had Jack been too forthcoming with Skiddy about the identity of his landlords in some passing comment about the injustice of this dog-eat-dog society? Had Skiddy blabbed the extent of the Overends property portfolio to someone up in The Long Hall who had in turn blabbed it to Bizniz? He shouldn't think so badly of Skiddy. Whatever their differences they existed on an ideological level. He was entitled to his beliefs. Why should Skiddy, a beneficiary of the shelter it provided, do something to jeopardise the survival of the poetry collective?

- Are you alright?
Jack started as he looked up from the letter to the face of Kate Keane.
- Kate...fine!
- Jack, you don't look fine. Has something happened?
He looked around the room to see if anyone was looking, then silently, he passed the summons to her. As she read, he noticed Skiddy looking at them.
- I'm going for coffee in the The Kingfisher, if you'd like to join me. It's not very easy to talk here.
Skiddy was now looking more intently at them. Kate seemed unbothered by this, but in deference to Jack's discomfort, she moved off.

Jack had actually found Skiddy more friendly since the vote, probably because Skiddy had had his way over procedures. He had even called up to the flat a couple of days before to see him. Why, Jack wasn't exactly sure, given their differences. Jack had arrived home to the sound of laughter. He hadn't heard Rosa laugh like that for such a long time. Ascending to the kitchen he found Skiddy doing a perfect imitation of Paddy Jenkins. Rosa had stopped laughing all of a sudden as Jack walked in. Skiddy hadn't flinched and Rosa, unable to contain herself, had burst out laughing again. Jack thought it a rather forced and desperate laugh. On completion of the story, Skiddy had presented Jack with a book he had been meaning to return to him for months. Jack looked at the Patrick Kavanagh collection, jacket now covered in coffee stains and encrusted grime, while trying to remember lending it to Skiddy in the first place. He'd been looking for that book everywhere since its disappearance from the shelves of the Poetry Collective. What did it matter? Skiddy had at least read it as evidenced by his repeated quotation of the closing lines of On Raglan Road.

The visit left Jack with an uncomfortable feeling. He found himself thinking of an event in his childhood when he had answered the phone to his mother's lover, an affair of which his father remained oblivious. Jack had been surprised to find the interloper enquiring after the whereabouts of his father, but ever keen to oblige, had promptly responded to the enquiry by calling out to his father, only realising as he released his name that what the interloper had been asking of Jack was whether the coast was clear or not. Jack had stayed on the line listening to two grown men talk about the lawnmower one had loaned the other when what was really being discussed was his mother. While he subsequently absorbed Plato and his world of forms hungrily at university, he would always identify this unusual conversation as his introduction to metaphysics. When does a lawnmower cease to be a lawnmower. When it's your mother of course.

As the sun dipped behind Dominick Street flats Rosa grew silent in the ascending gloom, the cries and laughter of the children on Granby Lane gave an edge to the tension between them. In an effort to break the silence and still looking at the book, Jack observed to Rosa how rough Skiddy had been with it. Rosa observed in reply how Jack hadn't even missed the book: it could have been sitting on his shelf clean and untouched for all he knew or cared. Jack said he knew someone had taken it from The Collective and didn't mind as long as they were looking after it. At which point Rosa accused him of always needing to have the last word and left the room. He felt guilty about having spoiled the good cheer of the party and even thought of going after Skiddy to see if he wanted to join them for a pint, if that could have restored the laughter to her voice.

He didn't understand why she was so upset, but things had continued in that tone. Afraid to speak in case his words be deemed wanting to have the last word, silence descended between them. That morning, in an effort to break the ice he remarked to her casually about waking up to a sharp pain in his foot and finding a splinter of glass that had not been there when he went to bed.
- Good!
Rosa's response took him by surprise.
- What's that supposed to mean?
- I'm glad you found it.
She looked at him accusingly.
- Now I suppose you have no idea how that got there?
He awaited the answer to her question. Her expression was tired and drawn as watering eyes examined him. They remained staring at each other for what seemed like an age, when out of the blue it came.
- Jack, do you love me?

He remained staring at her blankly as if he hadn't heard the question. Why was she asking him this now? Was she trying to distract from her insensitivity towards his sore foot? She'd never asked him before. She was normally so sure of herself. The question sounded corny. She was just trying to change the subject

     - No, Rosa...

He saw her face drop, but this didn't stop him.

     - ...I don't know how that piece of glass got there.

Then she got up and was about to leave the room when she turned and looked at him with accusing eyes.

     - Of course you don't. You don't have a clue, least of all about yourself.

As he moved around the house in the wake of her departure for work, he kept finding these messages scrawled on bits of paper and stuck to the wall: "conceived in the bath (or a watery bed perhaps), born in the air", "the hermaphrodite lying in the dark needs light". Jesus, Rosa was losing it. She needed to stop working in that mumbo jumbo shop and the sooner the better. While he was keeping it all together, she was losing it.

The collective had gone silent, cleared by Skiddy's outburst. Arlene had gone for coffee, taking Skiddy with an offer to sub him until he got some cheque or other. Skiddy had her wrapped around his little finger. Jack should really take her aside and warn her, but then that might seem like sour grapes over her siding with Skiddy over Policy and Procedures.

The early afternoon sun was making its way into Granby Lane. The city was a far off hum, but for the sound of buses revving on the Square. It occurred to him that he had done little to progress his poem for the competition. He had been preoccupied with doing everything else other than what he should be doing. He remembered that Kate was probably waiting for him in the Kingfisher to discuss what appeared to be their imminent eviction. Shooting the breeze with Kate for half an hour was an attractive prospect. He always felt a sense of well-being in her presence. He could talk to her about ideas, even the idea he was now considering to compose for the competition. She was always so considered with her responses. After all she knew what it was like because she was a poet. Maybe this was where life with Rosa was foundering. He didn't know what Rosa aspired to be and therefore didn't know how to encourage her, how to love her.

Before he could talk to Kate about his poem he had to have something to show first. Having something to show her seemed to matter more at that moment than having something to show Rosa. If only Rosa were a poet. She knew a lot about poetry but had no interest in writing it. He pulled his notebook out of his bag and looked at the heap of notes he had scribbled. They all referred to the encounter with the fallen scaffolder on the pavement outside the building. The weird moment as the man looked him in the eye like he knew him and revealed his identity, him out of all the other passersby. He realised this was an epiphany of sorts. Though he couldn't divine what this epiphany signified he knew he was on to something as far as his poem for the Meaney Medal was concerned. He now had the title of his poem: "The Scaffolder Calls". Why not start his poem by describing exactly what he saw. He closed his eyes to picture the scene and opened them quickly and started to write:

> His arse in the air
> Face to the floor
> Like a ship run aground
> in the sand
> The traffic crawled by
> On Parnell Square
> His bus had long left
> From its stand

Without stopping to review, he closed his eyes to let the scene speak to him some more. When he opened them there was a man standing in front of him. He thought for a moment he had summoned up the Scaffolder, but there was no mistaking for Jack the bullet head and the rounded shoulders of his visitor. A feeling of dread enveloped him.

- Terry?!
- Don't let me interrupt you.

Jack instinctively covered up his papers while Terry Crowe circled around to look over his shoulder.

- Something to hide Jack?
- It's not finished yet Terry.
- I was talking about the hard-on in your trousers.

So there was. His mind may have been on the poem but his body was settling into a seat beside Kate Keane in the Kingfisher.

- Naughty naughty!

Jack ignored the comment.

- How's things Terry?

Now Terry ignored Jack, so he watched as Scary Terry Crowe dusted off a new set of spivvy clothes and sat down in the chair opposite him.

- I disturbed you Jack. You were deep in concentration there.
Jack nodded his head ruefully as the new lines he was about to commit
to paper were snatched away by the teeth of this deep-water pike.
- You're lookin' well Jack, which is more than I can say for this
kip.
Jack looked around the place with Terry's eyes. It would soon be history
anyway if Johnny Slaughter Jnr. was as annoyed as Jack thought he was.
- We're kind of broke at the moment.
- I know!
- You do?
Terry chose to ignore the question and instead pulled up a seat to take
a closer look at his former literacy tutor.
- And what about you, my old friend?
Jack ignored the question.
- Broke as well.
Terry cut him off again.
-       What about your creative soul?
Jack looked down at the page where his creation had stalled.
- Well I was just getting going on something when…
- I interrupted you.
Terry looked over his shoulder
- Is it about anyone I know?
- Just a guy I met.
- About me?
- No?
- You sure?
- Why would I Terry?
Terry seemed disappointed.
- Why wouldn't you?
Jack shook his head. He had never considered writing about Terry.
- It's just that I heard you were looking for me.
The aggression was already there in the voice.
- I just wanted to get your tapes back after I'd transcribed
them. I wasn't sure if that's what you wanted done, was it?
- It's a start.
Jack thought about the precious hours he had spent transcribing Terry's
tapes at the expense of his own work, but was more immediately
concerned by Terry's use of the words "yet" and "start".
- So what did you make of what I sent you?
Jack hadn't realised a critique of Terry's musings was required. Jack
moved to speak. Terry held up his arm.

- A bit of touching up is needed, I know. All in good time.
Jack wasn't sure what Terry was referring to and just as he was about to seek clarification Terry changed the subject.
- You know you owe me money?
Jack nearly fell off his chair.
- We do?!
- No, sunshine. You do! I don't deal with collectives. I want to see some personal responsibility, Jack.
Personal responsibility? This sounded like somebody else's words. Terry's probation officer perhaps.
- What money, Terry?
Terry went to another desk and pulled open a drawer. It was empty.
- You poets shouldn't be going around leaving debts behind you.
- We owe Alfie Bermingham for printing a couple of issues of The Bulletin...
- You owe him more than that. Heap of poncy shit!
- Oh have you read it?
Jack immediately regretted his mention of Terry's reading.
- What do you mean have I read it?
Jack felt these words of blame and thought Terry was about to crack up.
- I wouldn't wipe my arse with it.
He pointed the Bulletin in Jack's face and made him jump.
- Terry, if it's money you're looking for I don't have any, but I'll get some.
- That'd be too fuckin' easy.
- Not really but...
- Shut the fuck up. From now on you'll speak when spoken to.
Jack was all ears.
- Terry has a better idea.
Jack was relieved to have the awful silence broken. Terry seemed to calm and become more business-like.
- This country was once run by great chieftains...
- The O'Conors, The McCarthys, The O'Rourkes...
Terry nodded then held up his hand to silence him.
- And tell me Comrade, why do we remember them?
- Because they were great Irishmen with a sense of fair play and justice.
- Who said they were?
- Historians...
- And?

- Poets, Terry. Na filí.
- That's right Comrade, Poets. Every chieftain needs his poet.
Jack was beginning to get Terry's drift.
- Terry, I'll settle the debt.
- I want poetry.
- It'll take me a few weeks to get the money but I'll...
- You can be my Bard!
- No, I can't.
- I want people to read about me, about my children, my mother that worked her whole life down in the markets, hail rain or snow...about my auld fella sweating his bollocks off sweeping the streets for the stingy old Corpo. I want it there in black and white. I want to see you stand up in Conway's in front of the community, The Shinners, the women from the market and for you to read those poems and for people to know they're about me...
Terry waved his hand at the poem Jack had been writing and continued.
- ...not some useless fucker you might have bumped into.

Jack didn't like the work in hand referred to like this. What's more, he had never been commissioned before to write a poem, never mind a collection. So this was a surprise. This was why Terry had been sending him his thoughts and recollections since his cancellation of the literacy classes. He wanted Jack to write his life in verse. Jack already foresaw problems. Terry's father had indeed worked in the Corporation but had long given that up for a life of massive drinking and small time crime. Jack had to admire Terry's accurate understanding of the role of the praise poet, but where had he picked up this notion?
- Terry, I'll get you your money.
- From where? Now for every poem you complete in my honour, I'll debit your account at a pound a word. There'll be bonuses for rhymes, plenty of rhymes, I don't want any of this modern free form stuff you used go on about in my class.
With that Terry cocked his thumb and index finger in the shape of a gun.
- Now get writing, sunshine!
He released the barrel of his metaphorical gun and was about to head out the door when Jack looked at the half-written poem in front of him. It would remain half-written if he accepted Terry's ultimatum. He felt the words slipping from his mouth.
- And if I don't?
Terry swiftly turned and stared at Jack.
- You have a lovely girlfriend, Jack. Is she a poet too?

- No, she's not, Terry. She is definitely not a poet.
This Jack was sure about.
- But you always used to say that everyone is a poet Jack.
- Leave her out of this Terry. She's not a poet. I'll get you your poems.
- Plenty of rhymes.
- Sure, Terry!
- That's better, Jack. Terry to my friends. My enemies know me as grief.

Scary Terry, as Skiddy had named him, may have had a good appreciation of the role of the praise poet, but he knew nothing about the business of writing. Jack wasn't just some tap that he could turn on and off. Anyway, his attempts to pen an entry for the Martin Meaney Medal had been frustrated by too many diversions. Now Terry's arrival and his big demands threatened to set him off-course. He looked at his watch. Kate would have left the Kingfisher, disappointed perhaps. He could hear the others coming back from lunch. He gathered his notes and slipped upstairs to resume the task that Terry had intended when he first sent him the tapes: the life's story in verse of a modern day urban chieftain.

Jack might have done better to retrieve his own poem or to reflect on what had turned him into a lightning rod for every needy cause and individual that happened to pass his way.

VIII
Being Jack

City of canals and constant streams
Suspended between lake and sea
Your skies a halo of possibility
Your granite bed on which I dream

Skiddy woke with a start. Some mucker was digging up the road outside with a pneumatic drill and the sun was beating through the flimsy pink curtains that barely kept the sun out of this swamp of his that passed for a bed-sit. He didn't have the strength to get up and pull them closed. The place smelled like a bordello, the lethal concoction of various unwashed body fluids fermenting in the sun's searching rays. He debated whether to rise and fling open the window, but the damn thing was the one barrier between him and that pneumatic drill. His head was splitting, the scream of some prisoner in there trying to get out only masked by the drilling from the street. He focused on the upturned bottle on the floor. Had he drunk the whole thing on his own?

He contemplated going back to sleep and was trying to gather the fragments of the dream he had been having. Hot as hell it had been. He reached down to find that he was still hard. Calm yourself boy. No point encouraging any unnecessary blood flow to the head. He'd been dreaming about her again. La Bella Rosa, La Bellissima Rosa. They were in Galway. There was an audience. He was performing to an awestruck silence. Could this be for real?

The trail of destruction that had led him to this dreadful pass was slowly coming together. He was focusing further on the debris beside the bed, tissues, filters of cigarettes ripped from their tubes, a lump of hash, rizlas, a condom wrapper. Condom wrapper? So where were the contents of the condom wrapper? What had motivated the removal of the contents of same wrapper? More to the point, who? His eyes were taking a wider sweep of the room when he felt the hand move on his shoulder. He was waiting for the voice that might accompany the hand. He racked his aching brain. Who the fuck who the fuck? Start at the beginning. Retrace your steps, slowly. The taxi home from where? From a feed of bad wine. It could only be Suzy Street. Jesus he had

72

been in Suzy Street. Who with? Rosa, Rosa, La Bella Rosa? Can't be her. Not yet! He'd been dreaming of her, but not here in his bed, no way. Not like this. Who the fuck who the fiddler's fuck? It was coming back to him: art opening, the dreadful art, even more dreadful wine. Retrace your steps. Oh my fucking head. Relax.

Whoever this bird is, he could feel her body stirring beside him and a hand reach across him. He must have cut loose completely. He remembered that there was cause for celebration. He had a poem for the competition and he had his story for Bizniz, wrapped up. But who was this dame with the big wedding ring making up to him. Skiddy feigned a snore, exhaled and did his best not to panic, but the woman was clearly stirring. He could tell she was about to speak by the smacking of her lips.
     - Oh Jesus!
She moaned in a deep commanding voice he vaguely recognised.
He feigned a snore, buying himself some time.
     - I need to go.
Whoever she was, he hoped she would slip from the bed, grab a shower if she liked, be polite to the landlady on the way out and close the hall door, properly. Whatever had happened was not meant to mean anything more than this. That was Suzy Street. Whambamalam. The woman now rose above him, her body clearly stirred not by any urgency to leave but by desire.
     - Jack! Wake up!
Jack? What about Jack? Through his sleep filled eyes he could vaguely make out the outline of this strong featured woman. He fastened his eyes shut and rolled over, emitting a loud snore. Retrace your steps, fast.

The night-time city had been alive with word of Martin Meaney. The old commie was proving even more troublesome in death than in life with his coffin currently under detention in a warehouse in Holyhead awaiting the papers for his final freighting from Old Blighty. In the days preceding, every group of disaffected Paddies across the water had taken to the streets to bid farewell to their favoured son. The adulation for Meaney and the deep anger it masked over the continued incarceration in British Gaols of the Birmingham bombers et al had all become too much for the Brits, normally a tolerant race it had to be said. By the time the cortége arrived at Chester, stirring the passions of some Welsh holiday-home burning friends of Meaney, the authorities

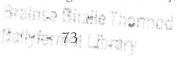

decided to hi-jack the body on the grounds of Public Health. Proper order. The poor fucker must have been melting after all the waking in Kilburn and Milton Keynes, Coventry, Leamington Spa, Crewe and every other ghetto of beleaguered Paddy migration. It was time to leave him home for burial before he leaked entirely from his box.

This was mourning on a scale that would have made Stalin jealous. Every miserable fucker experiencing the death of Meaney as if a nearest and dearest had passed away. For Skiddy this was one big juicy metaphor: life-long communist and revolutionary dies just as the great communist project crumbles to its knees. OK, he felt some sympathy for the plaster Paddies who lived isolated, leaderless and forgotten by their compatriots in the homeland. As a Galwayman in Dublin, he knew what it was like to be an outsider. However, the pronouncements of union leaders and lefty types with their calls for a national day of mourning were simply ridiculous. There had even been calls to halt all cross channel passenger and freight traffic to allow for the unhindered passage of Meaney's soul to the homeland. Get real losers. Meaney is only the first of you dinosaurs to cop it. Why should the economy suffer while you get wise to the defeat of your revolution? Anyway what about that trio of provos gunned down in Gibraltar? No day of mourning for them?

Meaney had already done wonders for the profile of Paddy Jenkins. He wasn't off the radio or the literary pages all week, waxing about "my friend Martin" and about "the university's proud expectancy at the imminent arrival of the poet's remains". Gas masks at the ready! It was obvious as the week went on that Jenkins was sounding a bit less sure of himself when it came to detailing the funeral arrangements. The battle for Meaney's remains had been joined and rival mourners were sharpening pen and elbow ready to beat their way to the graveside.

The task of identifying Jenkins' opponents, set him by Donal Don't You Know Dolan, had not been easy. This key rival had proved a difficult fish to name never mind catch. Information had been gleaned in a maze of art openings, poorly attended poetry readings, after hours drinking dens. The gallons of bad wine, slops for pints, whiskey chasers and hash had now been distilled into a story he could stand over and which he would deliver to D-Donal Don't You Know Dolan in the morning before delivering his poem for the competition.

He had conquered some of the hardest drinking dens in the city, Mulligans of Poolbeg Street where the Irish Press scribes were firmly against the Jenkins faction; on to the Irish Times Club on Wellington Quay where Jenkins, as a regular contributor to the paper's literary pages, was definitely in favour; Doheny and Nesbitt's where the political class were urging the Taoiseach to put some order on the unseemly tussle; and finally to the doors of this cloistered establishment of aesthetes at which he had been reliably informed Jenkins' rival biographer would make an appearance.

He looked around him at the low chattering wine-swilling doyens of the The Arts and Literary Club (of Ireland), or "Alcos" as they were known by friend and foe. What exactly you had to do to become a member Skiddy was unsure. Artistic prowess was certainly not a requirement, judging from the art show that bedecked the walls of the bar and which had been the object of this evening's self-important soirée. The mediocre pastels of familiar Dublin street scenes, bereft of people, would have looked more at home hanging from the railings on Merrion Square. The throng had allowed him infiltrate this normally secluded snug unchallenged. But now the crowd was drifting away and there was no sign of his quarry.

They were a voluble lot, among them voices he recognised from that soporific Sunday morning literary show of reminiscences that he treasured so much for its capacity to put him back to sleep. There were a couple of stage actors he recognised from boring boyhood soap operas. One of them, a former beauty who had shocked 1960s Ireland with the first televised full on-air kiss was now concealing her age with a remarkable blue rinse hair-do arranged in a horrendous 1950s perm. There was a red-faced barrister from up the country who had dutifully opened proceedings and had bought a few of the paintings from the artist who appeared to qualify as a member of the club for reasons other than her painting, clearly a side-line.

His tip off had reliably informed him that the man who had been anointed by the Meaney family to give the graveside oration two days hence would make an appearance. The Arts and Literary Club was his port of call when he hit town and this lot were his set. Indeed, the name Uinsionn OFlatharta had been doing the rounds in hushed conversations. The celebrated Conamara poet of poets, leading member of Aosdána (the self-selecting state-sponsored"wise tribe" of artists and poets) was a life-long friend of Meaney and was the putative author of the rival biography to which Donal Dolan had alluded. However, the star turn had not appeared and Skiddy was feeling cheated. All he had wanted to do was draw a few lines from him on the subject of Paddy Jenkins without revealing the purpose of his enquiry and to then get the fuck out of there. He also wanted to glean what influence if any the guy might have on the destination of the Martin Meaney Memorial Medal+Money.

Maybe he should just slip away now that he no longer had the protection of the crowd. There was only so long he could feign interest in the art on the walls. By the level of haranguing, in-jokes and back-slapping afoot, the remains of the gathering all knew each other. His outsider status and anonymity was still intact and he had learned all he needed to know about the identity of the man who was threatening to rain on Paddy Jenkins parade. But why hadn't OFlatharta turned up? He observed how their voices dropped in conspiratorial whispers as the sometime soap-star now appearing up at the Gate Theatre tottered off in the direction of the cloak-room still chattering to them as if this whole premises was her stage and rejecting entreaties from the red-faced MC to "have another".
        - The lady is not for turning.
She said in a deep throated commanding voice. It occurred to Skiddy as she passed him that the blue rinse perm might in fact be a requirement of whatever stage role she was currently performing and that Brenda Barron, wet-dream of many a bachelor farmer from the pioneering days of soap could still turn heads.

He observed the full glass of Piat D'Or in front of him and decided he would savour it while reviewing the poem he had drafted for the competition. Not the poem he had embarked on about Rosa which now lay in shreds in the waste-bin of the poetry collective, but a new more promising work. The poem for Rosa had defeated him not least because the mere thought of her was driving him to distraction. He had proved unable to separate the work from the subject. Any words he concocted paled beside the feelings of want for her. When it came to the poem he was unable to exercise that one quality that every poet needs: detachment. It seemed truer to him to expend his energies following through on these emotions, which he had done by calling around to her under the dreadful pretext of returning Jack's book. If only Jack hadn't turned up. Though he had brought joy to her face with his flirtatious banter, he couldn't help feel she was just playing him along to stir a reaction from Jack.

He had abandoned the poem for her but had not abandoned hope. Maybe he just needed to get Jack offside. In the meantime his growing contempt for Dublin with its insider ways and post-colonial airs, not to mention his feelings of being manipulated by Donal Dolan for his own ends, was threatening to make him quit the town altogether. All he could think of doing was jumping on a bus to Galway for a few days of sea air and tender loving care, while he nursed his feelings of unrequited love and worked out what to do with the rest of his life. He had even made it as far as the boarding gate in Busáras when he realised these were the emotions required to write a poem of promise: he missed Galway, but he also felt sufficiently detached from it. He was going back there with a plan to write a poem about it if only to forget about Rosa, but he knew that once he stepped off the bus the poem would never get written and he would start to pine for Dublin and descend into endless feelings of life is elsewhere, which of course was the poet's lot, the natural disequilibrium. It shouldn't be ignored, but explored. He also remembered that Galway was an even bigger graveyard for would be poets than Dublin. Within minutes he had re-claimed his position by the radiator in the poetry collective and was drafting his best work yet.

Tomorrow he would completely re-draft and weed out any silly rhyming or repetition of sentiment before the submission deadline. He would submit to Paddy Jenkins in person as he was still confident that although he was being challenged for the oration he would still be the arbiter of the Meaney Medal+Money. Skiddy was draining his glass when he heard familiar words being recited in a woman's voice. His poem? Brenda Barron had returned unnoticed from the cloakroom, fur coat pulled up to the gills, had pick-pocketed him and was deciphering his scrawl. Jesus. The eyes of the club were turning on her. He reached out to grab it off her, but she playfully stepped out into the centre of the room to recite his poem.

> City of canals and constant streams
> Suspended between lake and sea
> Your skies a halo of possibility
> Your granite bed on which I dream
>
> Your hidey-holes of would be scribes
> Tourist traps and student dives
> You taught me the meaning of I
> Lost city of the diatribes

Skiddy tried to interrupt but Brenda Barron raised a silencing hand.

> Your holiness will know no bounds
> While Taj Micheál commands the town
> And in Lent novenas will resound
> To renovate this hallowed ground

Brenda Barron cleared her voice for the final verse. Skiddy could not help his eyes seeking the comfort of the club's crested carpet. He wished he could climb into its deep pile.

> I am not lost but found in this alien town
> I dwell in a poet's no man's land
> And will not grace your streets until
> News of my election calls me down

He felt exposed, found out, unmasked, not least because the self-serving closing lines of the poem revealed his ambitions. If this lot were as clued in as he thought they were then he would soon be a laughing stock and any hope of seizing the prize would evaporate in the heat of their laughter.

- Name that town!

The red-faced barrister entreated. The names of various cities rolled out but the hints of Galway were strong enough if not completely fucking obvious for them to nail it.

If he could only just retrieve his poem and get the fuck out of there. Brenda Barron did not seem too keen to release it.

- Is it yours?

Enquired the admiring amateur painter. Skiddy started to shake his head. Brenda Barron still examined the poem. Had he signed it?

- S.K. Dee?

Christ, he had. Skiddy continued to shake his head. What was the point in owning up to it? If Jenkins got word of this he'd be finished. Consorting with the opposition. Anyway, a real poet would wait till he had put the bloody thing to bed before committing his signature. Such vanity.

- Identify yourself!

Brenda Barron instructed in an assumed deep throated voice, possibly that of the role she was currently performing up at the Gate Theatre. The blue rinse was beginning to make a bit more sense. He had often thought of being an actor. Why not?

- Jack…Jack Lennon. How do you do?

There it was. He'd done it. Stepped into another's shoes.

    - Well Jack, what are you doing with this freshly scrawled poem by one S.K. Dee?

Good question. Now, could he carry it off?

    - I'm an editor of a poetry pamphlet.

The others who had been drifting back to their banter sat up.

    - Which pamphlet?

The red-faced baritone barrister demanded.

    - The Monthly Poetry Bulletin.

    - Never heard of it.

Good he thought. You'll never hear of it again.

    - Oh, we're a poetry collective.

Collective. It pained him to say it, but they seemed to accept it. Worthy and anonymous. Great. Red Face was drifting back to the trough. Skiddy was home and dry. Almost.

    - Well Jack, what brings you to an art opening if poetry is your metier?

Enquired the friendly but searching Brenda Barron. If only her taxi would arrive, the interrogation might cease. He smiled at her while gesturing to the art on the walls.

    - I'm a poet, you're an actress. Why not?

    - A young man like you must have more exciting places to be.

She squeezed his arm reassuringly. Where do you have in mind? he thought to himself, but then remembered his mission.

    - I was hoping to meet The OFlatharta.

A stony silence descended, glances exchanged. All eyes then turned on him. Brenda Barron loosened her grip.

    - What makes you think he was going to be here?

Red-face intoned. He had to think quickly.

    - It was on a press release.

    - What press release?

Accusing eyes now turned on the bird-like artist who had obviously over-sold her opening. She was about to enter into explanation when Skiddy silenced her with a commanding gesture of the hand.

    - We only wanted to know if he'll deliver the oration or not, for Meaney?

He felt their looks of suspicion. If they had an inkling that he was there in the service of Bizniz, the authors of the "alco" acronym, they'd have him in the cellar for interrogation.

    - Why wouldn't he?

Red Face demanded.

    - So, he is then? Great.

          - The wishes of the family will be respected.
He could sense their suspicion of spies. If he left now, it might look like
panic and one phone call in the morning would expose him. He started
to turn his empty glass in his hand.
          - You better stay.
Red-face lifted the bottle conspiratorially in Brenda's direction, much to
the dismay of the bar-man who had been suggestively clearing the
decks. The interrogation of Skiddy had given them the necessary
leverage.
          - Oh why not? I was only rushing home to feed the bloody
cats.
Brenda relented, accepting the fresh glass from Red Face who only then
lifted the bottle in Skiddy's direction, fixing him with an interrogator's
eye as he poured.
          - What exactly do you wish to know about Uinsionn
OFlatharta?
          - Well, he's the obvious choice for the oration, but…
          - But?
          - We took a visit from some fellow called Jenkins a few days
ago. He seems to have some claim on Meaney's legacy.
          - I'm glad you told us Jack. That man is a failed poet.
          - Precisely.
Skiddy supped deeply.
          - He's not a poet of any sorts.
Dorothy, the pretend painter, opined. Cat calling kettle.
          - Have nothing to do with him. The man is a complete
impostor.
Red Face concluded. Skiddy pressed on. Being Jack was proving useful.
          - Well that's what we thought, but he seems to be well
connected.
          - Not as well as The OFlatharta.
Brenda Barron re-joined the fray.
          - Oh?
Skiddy awaited elucidation.
          - What did Jenkins want, Jack?
          - He's running some competition in honour of Meaney.
          - Charlatan!
          - West Britain!
Red-face impotently added. This was excellent. He had hit a gold mine.
Their blood was up. Another bottle was produced.
          - If OFlatharta is as well connected as you say he is, he won't
get away with it.

Skiddy opined.

- Precisely Jack. He won't. He cuckolded poor Meaney. He was broke, he didn't know what he was doing and gave him all his papers, the lot.

Skiddy fell back to listening and ordering his story for Bizniz while they poured forth on Paddy Jenkins, how he had succeeded in convincing Meaney's relatives to let him deliver the funeral oration as a prelude to writing the biography of Meaney. In response, OFlatharta was going over the family's head this same evening in a visit to the highest of the high. The country might be falling apart but its leader, the Taoiseach himself, took a big interest in the Arts, dispensing patronage from his own office. With this among other nuggets being gleaned Skiddy knew his story was moving fast up the running order for this week's issue of Bizniz.

Brenda Barron picked up on his increasing composure and she withdrew from the bickering to become more attentive towards him. When her taxi came she sent it away. The wine flowed and then Skiddy gave his apologies. He could feel grateful eyes lift towards him as he stood to his feet. He had given grist to their grudge and purpose to a bout of binging that had earned them their Alco reputation.

Skiddy waited on the front steps of the Arts and Literary Club of Ireland as long as it would take him to finish his fag. It didn't matter that Uinsionn OFlatharta had not appeared. He now had the story of just how high up this feud was reaching. He wasn't even half way down his smoke when she was standing by his side. He had completed that picture too. Brenda Barron was currently appearing in the lead role of Margaret Thatcher in the Gate Theatre production of Jaded, the West End hit of 1988. As she joined him on the steps, he examined her. She might be twenty five years his senior, but she was far from Jaded. Still, he couldn't quite get his head around the notion, not least because the woman had a husband in addition to the cats about which she had earlier fretted. But now was not the time to quit. He had his poem and he had his story. She seemed to read his thoughts and together they uttered the words that spelt further debauchery.

- Suzy Street?!

IX
Sub-Rosa

The shop had been quiet for most of the morning. Rosa was seated at the window of the Alchemist's Head like Ariadne, weaving her web. She watched as an elderly American couple wandered up Essex Street, strays from last week's Saint Patrick's Day celebrations. Stopping outside the Communist Party bookshop, the decidedly old and bedraggled looking New Books, they were probably taken by the more populist titles of romantic Irish national triumphs in the shop window and ventured in. Inside they would have been treated to more hardcore fare of the Collected Works of Lenin, Marx, Stalin and Ireland's very own communist thinker James Connolly; pamphlets excoriating US Imperialism in Latin America and treatises trumpeting The Crisis of Capitalism in Ireland (which Jack had tried to convince her was on its last legs).

Moments later the tourists stormed out of the shop and crossed the street as if they had witnessed something ghoulish. For Rosa no one could be more inoffensive than the Spanish Civil War veterans who ran the shop. She didn't really think of them as communists, but more as Romantics in the great European tradition.

The couple had just about cooled their heels by the time they reached the Alchemist's Head and responding to its more quaint exterior had wandered in, greeting her with a big, if nervous "hi...no communists in here?", followed by an equally nervous laugh. "Not yet" she had replied without irony. This was met by a relieved "great", in the belief they were all of a mind. However, their friendliness was short-lived as she thought she heard the lady lean over to the man and utter one word: "witches". This was enough to make him replace the Tarot cards he had thought quaint but "missing a leprechaun" and to send the pair of them in the direction of the door without so much as a "have a good day".

Good riddance. The visitors had distracted Rosa from what was proving a compelling rectification. Since her early practice of compiling birth charts Rosa had become expert and it was not unusual for people to ask her to do their charts. Sometimes, she just did them out of curiosity. They could be great sources of information and guidance. But the chart in front of her was troubling her. The further she went into it the more uncomfortable she was feeling. She drew back from it, reminding herself that what she was involved in was a vocational exercise: the application of an ancient practice with which to gain knowledge of a person's place in the universe. She always tried not to project herself into the chart on which she was working. But this one was proving difficult. She looked at the heading.

Rectification No. 235. Stephen Kieran Dee. Born 6.20am, 5th November, 1961, University Hospital, Galway.

Scorpio. What else? Always the sting in the tale. Mars ascendant, Pluto descending. All very predictable really. Stephen Kieran Dee. A warrior for his own cause. Pluto, the darkest of the planets providing a brooding quality that could be interpreted as shyness.

The files of the Poetry Collective had provided Skiddy's date of birth, but to ascertain time of birth she had taken the step of phoning his mother in Galway pretending to be from the Sunday Independent and carrying out a survey of the birth signs of our up and coming poets. A thrilled Mrs. Dee had been very forthcoming. In fact Rosa had encountered difficulty getting Mrs. Dee off the phone. The woman had gone into detail about her Stephen Kieran's achievements as a child. When asked about his time of arrival into this earth she had elaborated in detail on the difficult birth. Stuck in the birth canal for some time it seems. That made sense. She told her too that Stephen Kieran was a vulnerable boy and that people should be mindful of the great talent they had in their midst.

Vulnerable? Perhaps behind all the bragging and brooding there was a shy and insecure individual. However, it was clear to Rosa that this aspect of Skiddy was clearly being suppressed and that the Red Planet would remain ascendant for some time. Pluto's weak light might never be allowed to shine if Mars remained ascendant. But was Skiddy really trying to nurture his gentler side? Was there really substance to the things he had said to her in the kitchen before Jack had arrived back to find them laughing? He had a slippery serpent's tongue and it would be a lie to say he hadn't turned her on. Then again, she recognised that in her present state of abstinence, it didn't take much to turn her on.

She needed to take a break from this. She needed air as she was experiencing the mildly claustrophobic if horny sensation she had felt as he came onto her in the kitchen before Jack's arrival. He hadn't quite propositioned her but it was clearly on his mind. She had managed to keep him at arm's length and he had acquiesced, preferring to entertain her with his very accurate imitation of Paddy Jenkins. It seemed he had been doing research into Jenkins and had what she thought was a perceptive reading of Jenkins' self-serving character. He inevitably brought the subject back to sex by asking her if Jenkins had ever tried it on with her as he seemed to admire her. Rosa had said he hadn't needed to as the bimbos in the class were more than ready to give him their attention.

She should never have initiated Skiddy's chart. She had to remind herself that this was the young man who tried to stick the knife into Jack at every turn. Jack had told her once about Skiddy's menacing phone calls and how he had gotten his brother - an actor in New York - to phone Jack in the middle of the night to proposition him. Perhaps Skiddy had mistakenly identified Jack's hermaphroditic condition for homosexuality. Another time, Rosa had wandered into a pub to find Skiddy satirising one of Jack's poems. This snake was now wriggling his way into her life. She convinced herself that the means to head the snake off rested in his chart.

Rosa locked up and left a note to say she would be back in ten and wandered up through Temple Bar to buy a newspaper, passing the familiar sound of sewing machines from the first floor sweat-shop on Crane Lane, along by the steep walls of the Olympia Theatre, dead in these daylight hours; much more lively in the wee small hours in a town that still observed Victorian licensing laws. Two raps on the side exit could see to that.

While waiting in the shop on Dame Street one of the prostitutes from the brothel on Eustace Street was relating to the shop assistant about a raid by one branch of the police on a pub that was owned by members of another branch of the police. The back-lane pub was a haven Jack had told her for the after-hours drinking by members of the force. In the shop assistant's opinion, the area was due a bit of a clean up. The prostitute asked her to elaborate.

As Rosa wandered back, she wondered if Jack had ever gone with a prostitute or to what extent he thought about other women. A sense of panic came over her as she considered the possibility that there was someone else. If there wasn't what did he do with the pent up sexual energy? Did he just bottle it up? Had he become proficient at the hermaphroditic practice of transforming these energies into philosophy and imagination? His work, which she noticed had been deteriorating, didn't suggest this possibility. Perhaps his mind was on another, such as Kate Keane?

Rosa longed for the directness of Skiddy, and for Jack to learn to take her in hand. Was she being guided towards Skiddy? It felt like that. It might never last between them. A Scorpio like Skiddy would ultimately obey the instruction of Mars and try to destroy her. If she let him. Was she ready for this darkness? She had become a creature of the night. Then again, it was Jack who had turned her into that, not Skiddy. It was Jack and the sense of absence he created that was inspiring her craving. Or perhaps he was the expression of her craving. The nights with him as she joined him in his sleep-walking had opened up all sorts of possibilities. It was only in these nights that she had really begun to write.

She seemed to be having the complete opposite effect on him. It all seemed to be going horribly wrong for Jack. Last night as she had put her own work to bed, curiosity had got the better of her and she had uncovered the folder of recent work that she noticed he had been concealing furtively under lock and key. Four poems written in the most puerile verse she had seen in a long time. This was not his style. Too much naive rhyming for a start. A self-pitying voice that had replaced the usual passionate if impersonal tone of his work. Other forces had clearly started to work through him. Dark forces. This was the work of an unhinged mind with talk of violence and of vengeance. Perhaps his darker side was beginning to emerge, which was promising. However, the results were depressing.

As she had been reading through the work he had risen out of the bed behind her to begin his sleepwalking. She had un-tethered the string from around his ankle, which she had employed since finding him on the roof. Now, as he walked he started to speak in the voice with which she had found him speaking some nights before. "You are now part of my tribe..." It was not his voice, but a low awful drawl. "Which tribe?" she had tried to coax out of him. "My wise tribe", he had answered obediently, before opening the door to the street. "Who are this wise tribe?", she had sought clarification. She couldn't figure how his work could be so dark and downright bad if he was in the service of one of the wiser tribes. She repeated the question: "Tell me, who are this wise tribe?" "Bunch of lousy cunts", he replied. This made more sense to

Rosa. This was not Jack speaking. He never talked dirty. "Who Jack? Who are these lousy cunts?" With this he started to recite.

Abandoned by that lousy bunch of poets to my hell
I am alone in this icy six by eight prison cell

So this is how he saw their bedroom! All this sleepwalking was about his desire to escape. It wasn't the bird of his imagination trying to break free. It was an effort to escape her.

As Rosa wandered back to the shop she thought, with regret, about her asking him if he loved her. She should have just told him straight to his face that he was a hermaphrodite and as a hermaphrodite probably incapable of ever loving anyone but himself if he would only just admit it.

Tonight, they would talk straight the way they never talked straight. She would get the answer she needed out of him one way or the other and leave him to deal with the fact that he was in the grip of supernatural forces, whoever this tribe was. However wise they were, his work was deteriorating under their influence. New forces would have to be invoked. And if he was going to start talking dirty could it please be to her and nobody else.

She hoped that he would be waiting at the shop when she got back. There was someone else waiting outside the shop. Someone she hadn't seen for some time.

Janette Marshall must have felt Rosa's examining eyes, as she shifted a little unconvincingly with an annoying foot-scrape on her shiny black high-heel boots. She didn't have the legs for the black lace stockings or the hips for the mini-skirt, Rosa thought. However the black silk shirt and designer leather jacket saved the day, black eye-liner the one remnant of her goth days. She swung her briefcase in her right hand as Rosa approached bringing it around as if to shield her low-cut skirt and knobbly knees from Rosa's examination.
        - Long time no see fruitcake.
Janette's best means of defence was always attack. Rosa didn't rise to it, opened up and walked into the shop. She thought she heard a hint of Sloane in Janette's accent. She had picked up more than flash clothes in London.
        - Well aren't you going to ask me in?

Janette persisted in defensive mode. Rosa didn't mind one way or the other really. She just didn't want Janette around when Jack arrived for their lunch appointment.

- Kettle's on.

She invited.

- Terrific.

Janette nearly tripped on her heels as she came through the door of The Alchemist's Head and looked, Rosa thought, contemptuously at the place, which Rosa realised hadn't had a lick of paint since their shared days here on No-Sex Street.

- What brings you to fruitcakeland?

Rosa decided to stir it back.

- Thought I'd drop in to see my old buddy witchy-poo.

Janette waited for a reaction. None came.

- How's lover boy? Gerry says he hasn't heard from Jack in ages.

Rosa didn't really want to get into telling Janette about Jack's latest bout of sleep-walking or that they were falling apart.

- I'm expecting him any minute. You can ask him yourself.

This put the heat under Janette as Rosa knew how Jack unnerved her.

- I'm here on business, Rosa.

Rosa remained nonchalant but threw an eye over Janette's outfit. What could she want?

- Yep! You're looking at a busy working girl.

- What has you so busy?

Rosa obliged by asking Janette the question she wanted asked.

- We're going to turn this whole area into Dublin's Left Bank. There was something so casual, but yet so convincing about the manner in which Janette said this.

- Who's we?

Janette handed Rosa a card which read: "Janette Marshall, Cultural Liason Officer, Left Bank Limited". Rosa didn't like the sound of this. The word "culture" had always been a dirty word for Janette. She had a chip on her shoulder about artists. So why was she peddling it now?

- But it already is Dublin's Left Bank.

Janette's shiny new veneer had already faded.

- I knew you'd be negative about it. Christ Rosa, the place is going to fall into The Liffey if something isn't done.

- But something is being done, the place was derelict a few years ago and now it's not.

She suddenly wished that Jack was here to do the questioning.

- Who's behind this?

Rosa demanded.

    - Behind it? Leading it.

    - Leading it then?

    - The Government.

    - The Government wanted to pull the place down and build a bus station and office block just last year.

Rosa replied.

    - Well they've changed their minds.

    - Why?

    - We convinced them. I convinced them.

    - Of what?

    - That culture is business.

Just like that. Well Janette's Daddy contacts went right to the top. Janette was now standing proudly in fencing pose scraping the heel of her fuck-me boots across the floor.

    - Rosa, we did what all those artists had failed to do with their dead-beat bleating. We stopped them building the bus station.

    - Just like that!

Janette sat up on Rosa's desk, crossing her legs flirtatiously, revealing the skirt cut to the crotch. Surely The Leader had been impressed by that.

    - More or less. Now we've set up Left Bank Limited and we're going to give the place a good going over.

    - What good will that do us? You know that will just push up the rents.

    - It's more a case of what are you going to do for us, Rosa?

Rosa was all ears. Janette continued.

    - In case you hadn't noticed, the big clean up has already begun.

Not only was Janette dressed like some Gestapo officer, she was beginning to sound like one. This cultural commando didn't sound very Bohemian to her.

    - The brothels, the sweat shops, the hippies, the spit on the floor pubs, not to mention those fucking Communists across the road will have to go.

    - This doesn't sound very Left Bank to me, Janette.

    - You'll be fine. Those elements are just not tourist friendly enough, Rosa.

    - Nor are we, Janette.

She thought of the two tourists who had fled the premises a half hour before.

- Well maybe you need to look at how you're marketing your product.

- Product?

- Exactly. You need to interface with your public more: tarot cards, palm readings, the odd séance for Chrissakes. I don't think you understand how marketable all this stuff is. You should see what they're doing in The States. The Occult is big business. Call it New Age and triple the price.

Janette had taken control of the place.

- Stuff like this.

Rosa realised Janette was now looking at the chart she had been working on all morning.

- Charts. Rectifications. Rosa, you could charge the plebs a bomb for this stuff; tourists twice the price. They're all searching for their true path.

- I don't do this for money.

- You don't? What's this one about then?

- Never mind.

Janette was studying more closely.

- Mars? Pluto? Now that's more like it. You know my Gerry's Scorpio too?

Rosa had forgotten.

- Yes, I did his chart for you, free of charge. Remember?

- I didn't know Scorpio was your type.

- Scorpio's not my type.

Rosa wanted to remove the chart, but Janette was studying more closely.

- You sure about that? Virgo paddling around in the waters of Scorpio?

That's more like it.

Janette had seen enough.

- Scorpios are deadly in bed.

Rosa ripped the chart from under Janette's nose.

- Virgo is trying to get out of there.

- Well at least it means you're getting something.

The situation required some explanation.

- No, Janette, I am not getting anything.

Janette had a point and she knew it. The two women exchanged looks. Janette softened.

- And that's why you're just doing a bit of research into this guy, is that it?

Rosa didn't answer, just folded up Skiddy's chart. The truth sounded really shit coming from Janette.

- That's how you ended up with Jack isn't it? You spun the web and finally he flew into it.

Rosa felt ashamed to hear the truth. She was relieved to see Janette preparing to leave.

- I think I already have the picture. If I were you, I'd give all this head stuff a break and try the Scorpio.

With this Janette picked up her brief case and exited.

- I'll be in touch.

As Rosa watched Janette leave, she rolled up Skiddy's chart and put it away. Janette's visit had disturbed her, not only for the neighbourhood cleansing operation she was planning but for the forthright reading she had provided of her relationship with Jack. Janette had come as a harbinger of the change that was not just about to be visited on the place she saw as her spiritual home but in the direction her life must take. She could not conceal herself and her dreams in this shop forever. She needed to talk to Jack about all of this.

Minutes later she heard the rattle of his bicycle on the cobble stones. What a relief Janette was gone. Rosa started to rehearse the speech she had earlier been running in her head about his hermaphroditic apparitions, about her needs and wants. She looked up expecting him to coast to a halt at the door. Instead, he just flew past the window like a bat out of hell.

Hoping him on some errand, she waited for him to return, but he didn't. Ariadne's thread had definitely snapped.

X
Feet of Feathers

Jack was shaking as he seated himself back to the wall in the cocktail cloud of sweat, smoke, pulses and pachouli oil of the Red Lentil cafe. He was almost fainting from lack of air and nervous exhaustion, the poems he had diligently written for Terry, still in his trembling hands. His scheduled rendez-vous with Terry hadn't gone to plan.

Across the smoky restaurant, now buzzing with well-fed bonhomie, Jack spotted his friend and printer Spider Sargent. Red Ink had their operation upstairs in this bustling collective which in addition to Red Lentil and Red Ink also included the Well Red bookshop. Spider was Jack's last hope of getting Terry off his back. Spider gave the seated Jack a comradely nod from his place in the food queue. Jack contemplated joining the queue, but he wasn't feeling hungry. What he had just witnessed up at St. George's Church had put paid to his normally shark-like appetite.

He needed time to think and for Jack there was no better place to think than in a crowd. While the Dublin Workers Collective had been experiencing some difficulties of late, this was not evidenced in the lively banter of the teeming cafe. The conversations around him were for the most part about recent bloody events in the north which had started with the assassination of three IRA Volunteers in Gibraltar.

The Dublin Workers Collective, or DWC, as it was widely known in the city, was a hot-bed of political intrigue. It had been set up in this tall narrow building some years before by a loose amalgam of anti-nuclear activists and national liberationists. Some of this cadre had belonged to a secretive, obscure and determined outfit by the name of The Revolutionary Action Movement. RAM as they were known to friend and foe alike were by now a largely defunct organisation, their energies focused on the collective commercial enterprise that was the Dublin Workers Collective.

RAM's new direction had come as a relief to left and right alike, not least because it had seen an end to their lunatic antics. If Spider Sargent's pole-axing of a cop on Anglesea Street at an anti-nuclear march around 1979 didn't put the lead into the Irish anti-nuclear

91

movement, the subsequent battering of the march by the cops certainly did. The same tactic would be used successfully a couple of years later at the British Embassy during the Hunger Strikes when a herd of pigs would lose the rag after a couple of hours prodding by some hard elements from up North. The truly brutal nature of the State, then teetering on the brink, was revealed to each and everyone of the crowd of 5000 marchers, journalists and ambulance men and women.

RAM had alleged connections to Red Brigades, one of whose operatives was suspected of the maiming of a British businessman as he lectured in Trinity about job rationalisation. One of RAM's leading lights Syd The Yid had scared the shit out of Jack one day by asking him for a loan of his passport. Lucky for Jack, his passport had been out of date and he was able to refuse Syd, politely. Rumours abounded, mainly circulated by RAM's many foes on the Left, that Syd was a Mossad agent.

The indication for Jack that RAM were no more was the cessation of their legendary journal Trouble and its replacement by a far more pragmatic venture in which Jack and his poets had taken a part. Jack had become aware of The Alternative TV Guide, an illegal if not particularly subversive publication, when Spider had approached the Poetry Collective one day looking for door-to-door sellers. Spider had explained that as most of his associates in the Dublin Workers Collective were known to the police because of past activities, they needed a cadre of "intelligent but anonymous individuals" to do the selling. Jack and his fellow poets had not taken kindly to the attribution of anonymity but had jumped at the offer. However, the whole collaboration had come to an abrupt end when the DWC was raided by the cops and monies owing to the sellers seized. Retrieving the money owed to them was Jack's last hope of getting Terry Crowe off his back.

Jack had barely managed four poems for Terry. The taped commentary on his life which Terry had provided, delivered in an often tearful drunken drawl had proved a hindrance rather than a help. The commentary had no form or flow. Finally, what Terry had provided as verse just didn't scan.

Jack looked up as Spider Sargent came to join him.
- I recommend the lentil soup.
- I don't have time Spider.
- Of course you do. I've got something upstairs for you.

Spider winked conspiratorially at Jack as he departed upstairs. Perhaps the money had turned up from their sales of the TV Guide. He wasn't going to get his hopes up. He looked at his hands and realised they were still trembling. He looked at his shoes. There were still feathers stuck to them after his encounter with Terry Crowe.

Only half an hour before, Jack had diligently set off for Saint George's Church to make his scheduled delivery to Terry. He had managed to produce four hundred words of the one thousand demanded. He knew this was going to take some explaining, but he was prepared to tell Terry that he was doing his best and that he wasn't some tap that could be turned on and off.

Locking his bike to the tall black railings of the church he had gained surprisingly easy access by the side of the building. The main body of the church with its modest pews, wood panelled walls and fine balcony was home to hundreds of scavenging birds, dwelling freely in roof, balcony and belfry. The air was full of feathers as birds busied building their nests. Bird-shit and encrusted feathers coated the pews and floor creating a glue that stuck to the soles of Jack's shoes as he tramped across the abandoned church. Saint George's was an appropriate den for Jack's avian master.

Terry was nowhere to be seen, so Jack ventured towards the stairs that led to the vaults of the church. Terry had told him once about stashing his ill-gotten gains there. Jack now descended with caution noticing how the coating of feathers and bird-shit on his shoes was padding the sound of his foot-fall on the stone steps. He heard the man's groans before he saw him. Thinking that Terry might have taken a fall on the steps he was about to speak out but thought the better of it. As he ventured forward to assist, the groan turned to a scream that filled the air sending the birds above him into a frenzy. The voice that followed was clear, recognisable and free of pain.
- That gear is mine, so I want my money?
It was as if Terry was speaking directly to Jack. A cowering Jack was confused. It was only at that moment that the bruised, bloodied and battered face of Terry's subject, who Jack recognised as another former literacy student Eddie Hennebry, came into view. Jack froze on the spot. He couldn't see Terry yet, but he was in no doubt that it was him roughing up the young man.
- I told you I'd have your money Terry, it's just the little fella's Ma isn't well.

- Boo hoo!

Terry moved forward revealing himself to Jack. His arms were crossed tightly. However, when he unfolded them Jack saw the gun resting on his shoulder, Bond-like. To Jack, Terry seemed new to guns.

- Shut the fuck up! Now am I right in saying you gave money for my gear to a person you should not have given the money to. Money that was owing to me and to me alone.

- Jimmy Dunne said you and him were working tog...

Eddie barely had time to finish his sentence before Terry's gun-wielding hand swept across his face with a bone-crunching whack which drew another gut-wrenching scream from the man.

- I told you Eddie, I do not want that man's name mentioned in my presence ever again.

Jack recognised the name of Jimmy Dunne as the one Terry had not wanted mentioned in any of his poems.

- Now, Eddie. You work for me and not the aforementioned. I supply the gear and you sell it at a commission.

Jack was horrified at the mention of "gear". Terry had even railed against drugs in his most recent tapes as the ruination of his community. Jack looked at the poems he had brought for Terry. They were full of his worthy cause.

From the Church above, Jack heard the sound of voices. Terry's lieutenants were approaching.

- Now Eddie, I have other business to attend to, business of the soul. So have I made myself clear?

Jack needed to get out of there, but he couldn't move without making a lot of noise. The combination of bird-shit and feathers had welded his shoes to the floor. All he could do was stand and listen to Terry's instructions to the victim.

- The sale of Jack Charlton mugs, scarves, football strips, hats, and any related football gear between Dominick Street and Gardiner Street is the monopoly of Terry Crowe. Seeing as we are in a place of worship let us pray that our recent victory over Romania is a sign of a successful campaign to come in Germany from which we can all prosper.

Jack thought he heard Eddie utter "amen". Under the cover of approaching footsteps, Jack untied his laces, stepped out of his shoes and prised them off the stone steps before dodging into a door-way to allow Terry's approaching lieutenants pass. Under the cover of animated conversation, Jack made his escape.

94

So Terry's gun to his head when he told him to "get writing" was no longer a metaphor. This was how he was now extracting debts.

Spider sauntered through the louvered saloon-like doors of the Well Fed café and surveyed the room as if he had forgotten where Jack was sitting. Jack noticed with interest the envelope in his hand. Spider's caution with the contents was encouraging. The Well Fed café was not the kind of place to flash wads of cash. The Special Branch regularly dined here on the look-out for visiting Republicans from the North. Spider stepped across the cafe, holding Jack's gaze svengali-like in his, sat down and clandestinely handed him the large envelope.

Jack was encouraged by its bulk, but thrown by the powerful smell of fresh ink emanating from it. Freshly printed money? Were Red Ink getting into counterfeiting? Counterfeiting was presumably why Syd had wanted his passport. Nothing was beyond them in the furtherance of the cause.

   - Go on! Take a look! Hot off the presses.
Jack prised open the sealed envelope. The rush of fresh ink made him even more light-headed. His eyes were watering. He felt the pages of a magazine inside. Spider urged him to "go on". Perhaps the money was concealed within the pages. Jack pulled at it and out came a freshly printed copy of Trouble Magazine - The Relaunch.

   - RAM are back in action, comrade!
Dolores and Spider exchanged warm glances across the restaurant as a speechless Jack started to flick through the pages of Trouble - The Relaunch in the vague hope that some money might drop out of them. Well at least things were harmonious in the Dublin Workers Collective after recent defections. Jack had to ask, now or never.

   - What about the TV Guide, Spider?
   - History comrade. It was just too much hassle.
Spider's tone changed.

   - You don't look too impressed. Look, we've got a double-page spread for poetry.
Jack spotted pages lifted directly from recent issues of the Poetry Bulletin.

   - What about this character Martin Meaney? Jesus, I never knew. What a revolutionary!
Jack felt guilty not responding to Spider on the subject of Meaney.

   - Spider, I need to talk to you about business.
   - The things he got up to. Even in his coffin, making trouble for the Brits.

- I was just wondering if the cops had handed back any of the money they took off the TV guide?
- Do pigs fly?

Jack persisted.

- None of it?

Spider dropped his voice.

- Well we knew Syd the Yid and some of the comrades were planning a breakaway so we'd stashed a few bob away.

- And?!

Jack's heart was pounding with expectation. He would happily go on a dawn to dusk commission-free selling spree of Trouble - The Relaunch if Spider could give him the answer he needed.

- You're looking at it, Comrade.

Even Spider could see Jack's disappointment.

Jack flicked through the pages again. Spider could see his desperation.

- Listen comrade, we reckoned that shared out amongst the sellers it wouldn't have amounted to much.

- How much?

Jack was fit to be tied.

- About a thousand quid.

- A thousand quid?!

Jack looked at the front cover of Trouble - The Relaunch which featured a photograph of a well-known thick-necked Lugs Brannigan lookalike from Pearse Street Station bringing his baton down on Dolores' shoulder.

- Bastards!

Jack heard himself say. A look of shock crossed Spider's face. He had not missed the hint of ambiguity in Jack's use of the word. A quiet humourless resolve entered Spider's voice.

- That's what we're up against comrade.

Spider stood up to leave. Jack was inconsolable.

Spider was about to walk away, when he stopped and wheeled around. Dolores caught this unscheduled movement from behind the counter. Spider caught her eye, then turned to Jack.

- I'm going to say it now comrade, get it off me chest. It's been a tough time for this collective what with recent defections. I think you could be a bit more supportive. We thought as a collective you of all people would be up for this show of solidarity with the workers and the nationalist people of the north.

As if able to lip-read Spider's words Dolores, revelling in the celebrity of her front-page appearance on the re-launched magazine, gave a supportive nod to Spider across the restaurant.

- Are we taking the wrong line or something?
Jack struggled to swallow a particularly large piece of carrot.
- The problem isn't your line Spider.
- Oh, it's not?
- The problem is the bottom line.
Spider dropped his self-righteous tone.
- Well, I'm sorry about that Comrade.
He turned to walk away and Jack stopped him.
- Spider!
- Yeh, comrade!
- The soup. It was very tasty.
Spider looked down at the empty bowl Jack had managed to polish off despite his anxiety.
- No problemo. At least we're getting something right.
Spider gone, Jack joined the rest of the Red Lentil café in a perusal of Trouble - The Relaunch, trying to find something consciousness-raising that would allow him see the big picture again. But he was unable to get the bruised and petrified face of Terry's minion Eddie Hennebry out of his mind. What pained him more than any threatened violence was the way in which the vocabulary of capitalism had crept into his discourse. Not only was he now enslaved to a rising north city gangster and about to be evicted by to the manor born Johnny Slaughter Junior but the ruling class that had turned Terry into this monster were now claiming his voice. He didn't care about the bottom line, but he cared about the Collective. The future of poetry depended on the survival of the Collective or so he had led himself to believe.

How had he ended up in this mess? What was missing that allowed the world come flooding in to wash away the things he treasured, including the poem for the competition that lay still-born in the bottom of his canvas bag. How could someone like Skiddy, despite being a believer in the capitalist ideology in it's most extreme every-man-for-himself Nietzschean form, still have his own colourful way of speaking and be able to dedicate his days to writing poetry and his nights to drinking and chasing other guy's girlfriends? What was Jack lacking that had got him into such a mess? One word. Self.

Skiddy, Jack realised, believed that he was the centre of the universe. Jack did not believe he was the centre of the universe, despite all Rosa's advice that "to know yourself is to know the universe". He was behaving like a survivor of some great catastrophe, undeserving of survival. Then again, he was a survivor of a catastrophe. His parents had disappeared off the face of the earth without warning. But that was small compared to the great disasters that other people had to endure. He couldn't quite think of one greater at that moment. And Jack was not other people.

All Jack's efforts to forget those sad events had proved useless. Grin and bear it hadn't worked. For one, he had been dreaming regularly about them. He'd even travelled in one of these dreams out to the place where they had met their death. Just as he was about to jump into the canal to save them he had woken up to find Rosa standing over him chanting. He had presumed himself dreaming of the candle-lit ceremonial scene that surrounded him, but now he realised it was for real.

This feeling of being out of synch dated from before his parents had met their bitter end. Were they a tragedy waiting to happen? Had he been stranded in this limbo because of their fractious relationship, trying to sow harmony where none existed? Or was it that he simply believed he belonged in another time and another place? Was it that he was trying to imagine another place? Another existence? Now this sounded like Rosa, with all her talk of parallel universes, past lives and after lives. Mumbo jumbo. But were his dreams of revolution not akin to some parallel universe? Revolution as some transcendental experience. The power to dream was the power to transform. He knew that Rosa was trying to draw him into this parallel world with her charting and chanting. Perhaps he should let her.

This was all running through his mind as he scanned the tribute to Martin Meaney in the pages of Trouble – The Relaunch most of which had been lifted from his obit for The Bulletin. There was one difference: where he had described Meaney as a poet who had worked as a fitter on the post-war high-rise project in Britain, the writer had taken issue with this "mistaken attribution". Meaney had indeed worked on the high-rise project, but not as a fitter. He had in fact been a scaffolder. Jack nearly choked on his coffee. Meaney a scaffolder. He thought of the man who he had encountered on the pavement outside his house. He thought of his unfinished poem for the competition. Dolores was on her way over to plamás him about the money. Not now. He had to get out of there.

As he wheeled his bike aimlessly up Dame Street toward Trinity College, he was reminded that Paddy Jenkins was due to meet his committee that night to select the memorial poem for Meaney. The thought made Jack sad. It made him angry. Being Terry's Bard had robbed him of the opportunity to prepare an entry for the inaugural Meaney Medal. And prize-money. The money. It was still sitting in Paddy Jenkin's top drawer waiting to be handed to the author of the winning poem: "from Haiku To Epic Form, the English language is the norm. Close of Business, March 24". Close of business? Jack checked the Trinity clock. Two-thirty.

He should probably go and apologise to Rosa for not bringing her to lunch as he had promised, but the day had flown and he only had a couple of hours in which to pitch for the award. He would make it up to her later. The judges were due to deliberate overnight and would inform the chosen poet before the memorial service. It was a slim chance, but if he could seize the prize he could have Terry paid off in jig time.

Jack had come to a halt without realising it, outside the Stock Exchange, corner of Anglesea and Dame Street. He looked up to the sky above him and imagined the scaffolder climbing above the city, bravely defying gravity. His instinct about the man on the ground on Parnell Square had paid off. This would be the most fitting tribute to Meaney he could deliver. Meaney the scaffolder. He had been prodding at the poem for days but now he had broken into it and it had him in its grip. He could explain everything to Rosa later. He would answer the question she had pointedly asked him about the L word, so stubbornly avoided. Why couldn't he just come out and say it? Did he feel undeserving of her love? He remembered something she had said which hadn't made sense to him at the time: "you should learn to love the world a little less and yourself a little more". She would understand if he now seized the moment to finish the poem about the scaffolder. For a moment it even felt as if she was right there at his side guiding him to the work.

In three minutes flat, Jack locked his bike to a lamp-post on George's Street before bursting through the door of Bewley's. At this time of the day the café was empty and the waitresses, the elders of the Bewley's fleet sent there to serve out their time, left you in peace to pass hours over one mug of coffee. He knew many of these ladies by name and they knew him. The catering machines were also the oldest stock, so even if the place was empty, there was always the racket of steam, crashing cups and trays being shunted to and fro, in and out of the washer, the perfect combination of solitude and industry in which to do some work.

Was his poem for the commemorative competition to be the last testament of a man condemned to the same fate as Terry's interrogation victim, of a poet writing for his life? If so The Scaffolder Falls might not only be his obituary in verse for Meaney but also his own.

XI

Ubermenschen Whores

A masterpiece. A complete and utter masterpiece. He repeated these words as he made his way through the labyrinthine corridors of Trinity's Lecky Building. Now, if he could just catch Professor Jenkins on his way back from lunch he could hand him the poem in person and make the necessary impression: he was committed to poetry and had nothing got to do with the exposé that was about to hit the newstands that evening, payment for which was now burning a hole in his pocket.

Donal Dolan had wet himself at the detail which Skiddy had laid on the bare bones of the Jenkins-OFlatharta Feud, embellished by the personal insights of Brenda Barron who had obligingly vacated his bed with a kiss on his sleeping brow that morning. No strings attached, not least because her actor husband was due back from tour that same day. It was Brenda who revealed to him the story of the woman the two gents had fought over all those years before and who gave the lie to the popularly held belief that this was a professional feud complicated by political and cultural differences.

Skiddy had spotted Jenkins in the Commons, late-lunching with some colleagues or perhaps his fellow judges for the Meaney Medal and knew it was just a matter of time for him to return to his office. He considered walking straight up to them to hand over his entry. However, he thought the better of it, knowing it was one thing to piss-off your fellow poets, another those who could be influential in paving the way to your advancement. He reckoned Jenkins would have to return to take a tutorial or attend to these beauties who were beginning to fret about their end-of-year exams. If it was Skiddy, he would have been back in a flash. What was it about these Trinity women, with their clear skin, healthy locks and fine voluptuous torsos? They belonged to a different race to the emaciated art students and stripling peasants he was encountering. An Irish Ubermenschen. But where did they go when they left Trinity? Did they just disappear? He needed to drink in The Bailey more, or start trawling the suburban hostelries of Sutton and Killiney.

Listening to these girls talk about the Poetics of Meaning or whatever it was they were jabbering on about, he realised what it was he liked about Rosa. Yes, it was that same self-confidence, the self-confidence bred by education. Education my arse. It was breeding. Genes. History. Power. Access. Everything he resented. Everything he wanted. He leaned over and asked the girls if Jenkins was due back. They suggested he ask the secretary of the department. A polite enough fuck off. Don't you know you're looking at the winner-in-waiting of the Martin Meaney Memorial Medal & Money?

Paddy's dogsbody Ms. Mabel Morris - as her name-plate indicated - was as well-spoken as the ubermenschen in the hallway. The same snooty Alex girls who were to be found in the back-rooms of that other self-important Protestant establishment, The Irish Times. An efficient sort this Mabel Morris, though· clearly up to her eyes with plans for the Memorial Service. Where was Meaney? Still in bloody Holyhead. Poor fucker. The department phones were alive with the same question. Yes, so and so would be coming; no, so and so would not be coming. He noticed her examining him out of the corner of her eye and took that as his cue to interrupt her.
        - I'm here to see Paddy Jenkins!?
He wasn't going to be treated like undergraduate scum, but Mabel Dogsbody was still reiterating to some journalist that we have no news of the attendance of Uinsionn OFlatharta at the memorial service. Yes we are well aware of his importance to the Meaney narrative. The word was out. Bizniz had obviously been leaking his article ahead of publication. Dogsbody put down the phone and looked at Skiddy.
        - If you're here on some special pleading…
With that the telex in the side office started to churn and Mabel Morris left her station to attend to it. While her back was turned, Skiddy whipped a couple of pages of Trinity headed paper from her desk. Never know when he'd have to write himself a reference or fake a letter to the dole. He also noticed a list of seat reservations for tomorrow's memorial service.

Back in the corridor he flicked through the list and confirmed OFlatharta's omission. More evidence. He'd be well covered when the shit hit the fan after this evening's publication. He was growing restless listening to the twittery. They weren't interested in poetry or smelly poets. They were interested in getting their exams and fucking rugger types picked up in The Pav, settling down in Killiney or Sutton after a stint going mad in London so they could have their Ubermenschen Kids.

He was about to tell them they were full of it when he heard the familiar tones of Paddy Jenkins one flight down. He touched the girls for a smoke, told his father had just collapsed and was about to go in and plead his case with The Professor. They didn't believe a word of it, but they were unaccustomed to being rumbled like this by peasants and obliged with the fag just to get him off their case.

Always take something from the situation was Skiddy's philosophy. It could be a story or a joke, a piece of headed paper, fags. If the subject could not provide with conversation, they could always provide in other ways. He ripped the filter off the Silk Cut Light and lit it off the remains of the cigarette in his hand as Professor Paddy Jenkins burst through the door, pursued by a gaggle of supplicants. Skiddy remained sitting.
   - Well you're the popular man today.
Professor Paddy Jenkins recognised Skiddy and came to a halt.
       - Ah!
He had forgotten Skiddy's name.
       - Stephen Kieran Dee. You look like you're busy Professor Jenkins. I just wanted to give you this.
Skiddy presented him with the envelope containing his entry for the competition.
       - I told you I'd have it for you. I think you'll like it.
       - It's really not up to me.
       - Of course not. I just didn't want you to think I wouldn't do it. There's so many bar-room poets in this town.
Jenkins smiled his weak smile.
       - Indeed there are. Now if you'll excuse me, Stephen...Kieran.
Jenkins signalled to his entourage, with an apologetic nod to Skiddy. That's better, Skiddy thought. He liked hearing the sound of his name on Jenkins' lips, even if it wasn't exactly rolling off the tongue yet, and to hear Jenkins excusing himself from his presence. He took a drag of his cigarette. How he'd love to see the fucker's face when he read the piece about him in this afternoon's Bizniz.
       - Not a bother. I'll catch you for a pint and a chat when all this is over, Paddy.
       - Yes, I enjoyed our last chat.
       - As long as you enjoy the poem Paddy. As you might say yourself, it's the work that counts.
Jenkins' nymphettes were looking differently at Skiddy now. That's more like it, he thought, as the Professor swept away. That stuck up cow who'd given him the cigarette to get rid of him sixty seconds before

even gave him the eye as she held the door for Paddy. Whore. Ubermenschen Whore.

As he walked back across the Front Square with the day lying at his feet, he was feeling good about himself and about the world. He had written the tat for DD, got laid, got paid and given the competition his best shot. Time to ring his mother and tell her he'd produced a great work and had just had a private audience with a Trinity professor.

- Operator, reverse charge call to Galway please.
This was worth an extra twenty quid in this week's allowance. His mother sounded well. She was impressed that he was phoning her from the precincts of Trinity. He told her about the poem he had written for Galway and even recited a few lines for her. He wasn't quite sure how he was going to get the subject around to money when his mother's words came like the sound of all the slot machines in Salthill spilling forth in symphony.
- There was a girl on the phone today wanting to know about your star sign Stephen Kieran.
Gotcha. The nosey little whore, he thought.
- "From the Sunday Independent?"
The Sunday Independent was God in the Dee household. He wasn't going to tell her the enquiry had come from some quack-shop.
- I told you Mam. My stars are looking up.
- Well done Stephen Kieran. You're obviously making a great splash in Dublin son.
- You better believe it, Mam. But we won't count our chickens.
- No we won't son. I'll light a candle for you this evening up at the Cathedral.
- You do that. And Mam?
- Yes, Stephen Kieran.
He couldn't bring himself to ask for money. He'd make do with the candle.
- Yes Stephen Kieran?
- You know you'll always be my number one chicken.
- Even when you're rich and famous?
- Even then woman.
- I love you too Stephen Kieran.

His mind was already racing. Rosa obviously thought that she was the one spinning the web. Au contraire. Au contraire. It was Skiddy who would choose the time and the place. This time she could not refuse him. And this time he would need to make sure that The Comrade wasn't going to come barging in.

Standing outside the gates of Trinity, he felt like the king of the castle. He took in the whole setting, this humdrum jumped up little provincial city with its pretensions to being other than it was. Not a real city, but a post-colonial, petty, provincial out-post. By tomorrow he would own the place. The city that "had sent poetry to the world", would lick his arse.

His eyes fixed on something up the street. Some idiot stopped still-life on the footpath just up from the Bank of Eire, causing pedestrians to walk around him and his bike. Was that The Comrade? Skiddy watched as the object of his attention gazed at passing people and traffic. He looked like he was losing it. Good. Skiddy had suspected as much. Something had to give. Suddenly the comrade seemed to break his reverie, turn his bike around and wheel it up the street in a manic dash. Fortune was smiling on Skiddy. He raised his arm regally to stop the traffic on College Green and set off up Dame Street in hot pursuit.

When Skiddy saw the comrade enter Bewleys, sit down and start to write, what he saw was a man clearly in possession of The Muse. This had to be stopped.

XII
Temple Bar

Rosa's sense of panic of that morning had begun to pass as she locked up the shop. Janette's discovery of Skiddy's chart had brought her to her senses. Things were going awry with Jack and they needed to talk, before things got any further out of hand.

An afternoon shower was now giving way to sunshine and the smell of grot and charred wood coming from the derelict lot beside the Project Arts Centre, the result of a fire allegedly set by a disaffected poet a couple of years before, was more powerful than ever. A handsome buddleia shrub was sprouting from the boarded up exit. The charred shell of the Project Cinema combined with the pock-marked condition of the cobble-stones that The Corporation had been busy plundering added to the sense of dereliction. Maybe Janette had a point. The area was in slow decline, despite the efforts of people to keep it together. But what was this tourist theme park she had planned for the area? Rosa was not sure she wanted to be around to see it materialise. At this moment in time, it was a quarter that was in the possession of artists and while buddleia flourished freely in its vacant lots there was a psychic energy about the place that was breathing new life into the city. Poetry lived here. It was like a spiritual lung for the city. Here, the forces of life and decay were engaged in mutual combat, but life was winning out. She thought how sad it would be for it to fall into the hands of a psychically and artistically retarded cretin like Janette and her Government sponsors.

At the information desk in the part of The Project that hadn't been burned down, the administrator - a fretful individual - was busy on the phone discussing an Aids benefit at which a number of Dublin bands were playing that night. Little chance of Rosa catching Aids in present circumstances. She made a donation and a silent affirmation for the Aids sufferers. Then she looked at some of the paintings hanging in the foyer by a painter called Pat Moran who kept a studio just down the street in an old converted textile factory called Maureen Buildings. The paintings she felt captured the melancholic feel of the city very well, but there was a warmth about them, an inner glow. One impressionist style painting entitled Temple Bar captured in the half-light of dusk showed some of the growing energy of the place.

- The exhibition isn't open yet!

The jumpy administrator barked.

- Isn't it?

Rosa turned with that look that could halt a runaway train. He should know her. She said hello to him every day.

- But you can come back later for the opening.

Came a calmed response.

As she walked up Temple Bar Rosa realised what it was she liked about this area, something which Pat Moran's painting had captured. It was a place to be young in a city that had never had such a place before. They were in the depths of an economic depression that had robbed the country of its youth. However, in the absence of economic possibilities the collective psyche appeared to be asserting its need for survival. Everywhere around her she saw youth and life. Viewed from the window of the shop it felt at times as if life was passing her by. She needed to be more adventurous. In these raw unformed surroundings there was a sense in which it was possible to try and fail, to reinvent oneself and not seem foolish.

She felt at ease with her decision, a decision which Janette's prescient visit to the shop and Jack's standing her up had precipitated. The poems written through the nights of sleeplessness in the Hi Brasil must see the light of day. Now, as she approached the corner of Anglesea Street and Dame Street there was something standing in her way. Stranded at the top of the street she saw Jack, halted, as if in some reverie. Despite her concern for him having missed their appointment, she found herself hiding in the cover of the Stock Exchange, while he completed the reverie. He must not know of her plans until they had been executed. Not least beacause she would feel the need to explain that she now considered herself a poet. In telling him she might lose confidence and change her mind.

Spying on him from the cover of the Stock Exchange she saw a face full of joy, even full of love, a face that he had never before revealed to her. Then, as if he had been spotted, he turned around and fled up the street. She was no less confused when moments later, another familiar figure, that of Stephen Kieran Dee marched up the street in Jack's wake. She saw this as no more than a positive sign that the two subjects of her competition poem "The Serpent and Hermaphrodite" had appeared to her in validation. Was it also proof of her suspicion that Skiddy's interest in her was a front for his interest in Jack?

Having handed in her entry to Jenkins' secretary Mabel Morris, Rosa returned to the shop and, feeling guilty for not having presented herself to Jack on the street, she set about trying to track him down; if only to find out why he had missed their lunch date. A frantic Arlene had answered the phone to her at The Poetry Collective. She had been barely articulate. There was only one decipherable word coming down the line from Arlene.

      - Terry!

Rosa tried unsuccessfully to calm her.

      - He's out!

Arlene continued.

      - Who, Arlene?

      - He's out and he was here.

There was only one Terry to whom Arlene could be referring, if by "out" she meant out of some institution or other. It had to be Jack's friend Terry Crowe, who had been imprisoned shortly before she and Jack met. Rosa encouraged Arlene to breathe deeply.

      - What did he want, Arlene?

      - Jack, poems and...

Arlene was now hyper-ventilating.

      - And, Arlene?

Arlene was apoplectic.

      - Arlene, snap out of it for fucksake.

      - "the rest of that tribe of lousy cunts"

Arlene burst into tears.

Rosa recognised those words: "tribe of lousy cunts". So, that hadn't been Jack talking dirty in his sleepwalking. That was Jack talking in the voice of this Terry Crowe. The tapes he had been listening to in secret were Terry's meanderings. So he wasn't in the possession of some Lost Tribe. Arlene had managed to stem her tears enough.

      - Terry said Jack had promised to do some poems for him and that he had missed his delivery.

Rosa instructed Arlene to calm down and directed her to the rescue remedy in their bathroom.

In further calls to Red Ink and to the call-box at home she had failed to find Jack. Finally, she phoned his Aunt Sarah, in the vague hope that he had contacted about his parents' memorial mass. Aunt Sarah told Rosa, somewhat possessively, that she had not seen Jack for longer than she could remember. Aunt Sarah was a retired scientist and the one member of Jack's large but fragmented family with whom he kept regular contact. She decided to ask her advice about the medicinal properties of Mercury and Sulphur. Aunt Sarah was aware of Rosa's interest in the Occult. Mercury and Sulphur were powerful elements in the hands of amateurs, she cautioned. However, she was perceptive and interested enough to understand the purposes to which Rosa might want to put these elements.

- So, Theseus is astray in The Labyrinth.

Aunt Sarah was a scientist with a poet's mind and liked to trade in euphemisms.

- Poor Ariadne. Leave Mercury and Sulphur where they are. You might poison him in a very noble but misguided cause, Rosa.

More than this Rosa couldn't do, until he showed up again. Moore Street yielded the ingredients for dinner and soon, the meal and the bottle of wine that she hoped would bring Jack to the point of seduction were awaiting his arrival home. This time it was his turn to phone. He sounded high.

- Jack, where are you?

- I don't know exactly.

Christ, he was in trouble. The journey she had predicted for him days before had now commenced. He didn't sound too concerned. While omitting her sighting of him earlier, she asked him straight out what the hell was happening. He said Professor Jenkins had contacted him out of the blue and had asked him to carry out a mission on behalf of the Memorial Committee. When she asked him what it was he said that a very important poet by the name of The OFlatharta was refusing to turn up for Martin Meaney's funeral and The Committee had decided Jack was the best person to send on a diplomatic mission to convince him to change his mind. This didn't sound like Jenkins.

- How did Jenkins find you?

- What does it matter, Rosa?

- Jack, I think you better come home.

- Rosa, OFlatharta is the most important living connection to Martin Meaney and his work. If he doesn't turn up it's a disaster.

Was he afraid to come home?

- Jack, are you in trouble?

- No!

He sounded way too defensive.

- Then why is Scary Terry Crowe trying to track you down?

- He is?

- Jack, you know he is.

- Don't answer the door to him Rosa. I've bolted the attic door and the windows. Rosa, he's armed.

- He's what?

- Don't worry. It's me he wants.

- Seems he's been looking for you everywhere and so have I. Now I can't believe if I or this Terry Crowe couldn't find you that Professor Jenkins could. The man is no psychic.

- Rosa, I thought you told him.

- Well I didn't.

His next words came like a blow to the heart.

- Rosa, it's better if you don't stay there tonight. I've left the city without any lights on my bike and this job may take time.

They had never been apart in their two years together. All Rosa could hear was the sound of traffic under Jack's breathing, not city traffic but the roar of fast moving cars, tractors and lorries. Mercury and Aphrodite sounded like they were on a collision course.

- Jack, just tell me where you are?

- Somewhere in County Meath, Rosa.

- You're what?

- OFlatharta lives out here, apparently.

- OFlatharta? I've never heard of him. Why now?

- Nobody out here seems to know him either. I'll ring you when I find out.

At that moment the line went dead. What a useless excuse for staying out all night: to lure this guy Terry away from the house? Why come up with this hair-brained mission to find OFlatharta as a reason for not coming home? Two words came to mind: Kate Keane. She'd seen the look of love on his face earlier that afternoon. No wonder she hadn't seen it before.

Rosa didn't have much time to dwell on this as moments later the door bell rang. If it was this Terry guy he was going to get a piece of her mind: armed or unarmed. He had obviously spooked the hell out of Jack. She thought better of answering the hall door and went into their top floor bedroom and heaved up the sash window, preparing to tell Terry Crowe to fuck off, under gun-fire if necessary. But it wasn't Terry Crowe standing there. The caller was one Stephen Kieran Dee, a bunch of flowers in one hand and two bottles of wine in the other.

- Anybody home?

Rosa knew that she should never have gone near his rectification.

XIII
A Return To Metaphors

Jack had not had much time to prepare for the mission that Jenkins had set him. Neither had he needed much orientation as he was aware of the circumstances surrounding Jenkins' relationship with The OFlatharta. This was one of the great feuds of modern Irish poetry. Poetry people of a previous generation had been split down the middle by it and no poetry gathering was complete without the threat of its painful eruption. The feud was running so long that people could hardly remember how it all started. Jack wasn't interested anyway. Falling out was such a waste of time.

However, it was an emotional Paddy Jenkins Jack encountered as he took the Bewleys' bakelite phone in his hand, having been summoned to take "an urgent call". Jenkins blurted out that it was time to heal old wounds with The OFlatharta and how fitting it would be for the reconciliation to take place over the remains of their mutual friend Martin Meaney. By the time Jenkins had completed his tale Jack had a lump in his throat. He knew that despite his discovery of The Self that afternoon, his mission in life was to bring people together. The health of the tribe depended on the healing of all feuds.

He asked Jenkins if the mission could wait while he completed his entry for the Meaney Medal. Jenkins said "whyevernot": he would collect Jack's entry "in person" from The Porters at Front Gate who would in turn hand Jack an envelope containing a peace note from Jenkins to The OFlatharta. Jenkins then asked if Jack knew how to find the OFlatharta. Jack said that he had had some dealings with him by post on Poetry Bulletin business, c/o Coon Post Office, County Meath. All he knew was that he lived somewhere in the environs and valued his seclusion. Jenkins, who it seemed was now barely able to contain his hysterical emotions said "thatwillsuffice". Before hanging up, Jack did manage to ask Jenkins how he had managed to find him and Jenkins had alluded enigmatically to "your all-seeing muse, dear boy".

On returning to his table, Jack could barely concentrate on his completion of The Scaffolder Falls. At least he had managed one pass before the world had come flooding back in. He was impressed by the obvious humility implicit in Jenkins' gesture and even more impressed that he had been the one elected to track down The OFlatharta. He revised the poem and re-wrote it in more neat script as he knew that he would be unable to make it back to the Poetry Collective office to type it up. First port of call, Books Upstairs around the corner in George's Market to ask Mossie if he knew where The OFlatharta lived. Wordlessly, Mossie had retreated to the back of the shop to follow up the enquiry. While waiting, Jack noticed that the latest issue of the Poetry Bulletin had sold five copies in as many days. Moments later the obliging proprietor returned with a copy of The OFlatharta's latest work, a slim collection entitled Between The Lines/Idir Na Línta.

Within minutes Jack had picked up his instructions from the cranky porters at Front Gate with an attached note on Trinity headed paper saying "Hermes, Make Haste!". The grumpy porter informed him that their office was for official university business and not some student half-way-house. Jack showed this uniformed little-Hitler the headed paper on which his instructions had been written before putting his entry for the Meaney Medal into the internal post marked "urgent".

He stopped by Conways and left Terry's poems in an envelope for him before setting off in the direction of historic Chapelizod. He felt the relief of being able to escape the city. He had made his pitch for The Meaney Medal & Money. For at least an evening he would be able to put Terry out of his mind. In this way he would be able to pick up the thread of his commission for Terry the following day. If The Meaney Medal & Money did not materialise he would have more work completed to show Terry.

At Chapelizod, he opted for the climb up the north bank of the Liffey past the back gates of the park. Then followed an exhilarating roll into the Strawberry Beds. Anglers' Rest, Wren's Nest and Strawberry Hall. He was already in the country. At Leixlip, he crossed the Liffey again and commenced the climb out of the river valley, joining the high walls and arborial splendour of landed estates on the run in to Maynooth. To take his mind off the exertion, he tried to recall what he knew about the life and times of Uinsionn OFlatharta.

OFlatharta had written his first collection Tír Chaillte (Lost Country) thirty-five years previously as an emigré in London, a tirade against the gaucheness of 1960s Ireland and the sell-out to multi-national finance. Civil Servant by day, hair-raiser by night OFlatharta was friendly with Behan, Kavanagh and of course fellow hell-raiser Martin

Meaney, forming the aforementioned London Poetry Collective. Before leaving London in the early 70s, OFlatharta penned his second collection Óige Chaillte (Youth Lost), a bitter-sweet adieu to the city in which he had squandered much of his youth on drink and women and on shrill political causes which did nothing for his poetry. It seems at this point perhaps the most traumatic event of The OFlatharta's life took place.

Despite exile he had maintained a fond attachment to his native island of Inis Raic (Flotsam Island), a small inshore island off the coast of Conamara. Travelling to his birth-place with an expectation to settle he found his dúchas deserted. Neighbours and family had abandoned the island in favour of the relative comfort of their newly built county council billets on the mainland. In a red rage he retreated to Dublin where he wrote the blistering collection Lost Island (Oileán Chaillte), an angry work in which the poet condemns his fellow islanders for their lack of resolve in the face of so-called progress and state inducements. His first publication in English and a satire on a fictionalised off-shore island which he called Inis Faic (Nothing Island), he forbade its translation into the Irish, a vengeful decision on which he would later relent while in dire financial straits. Critics including Paddy Jenkins hailed this work and welcomed him into The Pale with open arms, but he was of course condemned by his muintir and the Gaelic-speaking literary fraternity for a grave act of treachery in abandoning The Language. His harshest critics wryly commented that in his habit of losing the things he valued, The OFlatharta had finally lost his marbles. Facts become woolly at this stage, but it seems that the close bond with Jenkins was short-lived.

By tea-time Jack had reached Maynooth and the fertile plains of Kildare and Meath opened up to him. He had surprised himself with how much he knew about The OFlatharta and remembered that he and Skiddy had once had a long conversation about the poet in better days. Skiddy even had memories of him from his childhood in Galway, trading curses with the boatmen on The Claddagh.

Pausing to ask directions to Coon, Jack scanned the latest work of the Conamara poet who had now made an uneasy peace with his native tongue by alternating freely between the Irish and the English, a schizophrenia Jack believed had contributed the title of this latest collection, Between The Lines/Idir Na Línta. Jack smiled as he read a short satire by the poet in the English under the title "A Tight Corner", recalling that in addition to meaning "haven" in Irish, Cúinne also meant "corner", a subtlety which might be lost on the English speakers of Coon district. However, if translated for them by the local teacher or their countymen in the Rathcarn Gaeltacht, might mean that The OFlatharta had now fallen out with the people of Coon as well.

His lack of Irish was proving frustrating, particularly in his attempts to understand the title poem of Between The Lines that The OFlatharta had only allowed be published in the Irish. This lack of linguistic grounding might not only prove frustrating but fatal as articulated lorries breezed past him, honking their horns at his near invisibility on the darkening highway.

Jack was becoming disorientated in the gathering darkness. The pot-holed hard shoulder reminded him that the niceties of the city were behind him now and he was entering what Dubliners liked to call "the bog". Ahead of him he saw a weathered sign for a roadside restaurant. He could at least get some change for the phone and perhaps some directions to Coon. Though half-abandoned, there was something familiar about this restaurant which featured a large map at its entrance, indicating its position at the edge of the historic Pale. Sadly, the map didn't extend into Terra Incognita to allow Jack locate Coon.

Inside, the management of The Western Grill were slow to materialise. They hadn't even bothered to turn on the lights for the customers. While he waited, Jack scanned the bar and restaurant area, deserted but for a middle-aged couple dining in the gloom of The Grill with their three young children. Seemingly oblivious to the darkness of the restaurant, they had all the appearances of a happy family, their conversation inaudible under the rumble of traffic from the N4 western road. Suddenly, the lights of the restaurant went on and Jack was confronted by the spooked manageress.

     - How did you get in?

     - The door was open.

     - The restaurant is closed.

     - But..

     - I'm very sorry.

Jack turned to scan the restaurant and realised that the family who had been sitting there in the gloom of The Grill had suddenly vacated. What seemed strange was that there was no sign of anyone having dined.

     - We've been closed for the past three months.

The woman insisted.

- I'm only looking for some change for the phone and for directions to Coon.
- How are you travelling?
- By bike…

The woman looked disbelieving, until Jack pointed to the bicycle clips on his ankles.

- Well you best take the tow-path by the canal behind us here. That road isn't safe for you now.

The conversation with Rosa from the car-park phone only disorientated him even more. She had been so disbelieving of his story about The OFlatharta which was worrying given that he believed it was she had told Jenkins how to find him. However, as Jack cycled away he was convinced he had been in that restaurant before, a pit-stop on a childhood family trip west perhaps.

Now he was travelling alone. Despite the nearness of water and the failing light, Jack felt safe on the canal tow-path, heartened by the approaching lights of Coon. Up ahead he noticed a couple standing by the canal side. It was hard to make out, but it looked like the couple from the restaurant with the hoods of their anoraks pulled up over their heads. Their children were no longer with them. As he approached, they seemed to turn away from him, not wanting him to see their faces. He said "good evening" to them, but they did not reply. When he looked back again, he saw them walking away from him down the tow-path.

In the village of Coon, his worst fears were realised. Nobody wanted to know about The OFlatharta. A complete wall of silence. This crucible of fools had obviously turned its back on the poet. As he suspected, they had learned the true meaning of "A Tight Corner". Insulted by the poem, the small-minded people of village and parish had probably exiled the petulant poet. This was not promising. It was as if the poet didn't exist.

Jack climbed up out of the sombre little hamlet onto a tall stone bridge that straddled the Royal Canal and the accompanying North Western railway line. He hoped the bridge might provide him with a vantage point from which to spot cover for the night. The sun was on its last, catching the TV aerials of Coon and the tree tops of parkland beyond. There was no sight of the great house or castle that had once ruled town and parkland alike while guarding the western edge of The Pale. His eye was drawn to the last of the sun hitting the railway line, turning its steel rails a yellowy gold. Simultaneously, the canal beneath him was rendered a silver runway. Canal and railway stretched like parallel lines into the distance. Parallel Lines? Could these be the two lines to which the title poem 'Between The Lines' of Uinsionn OFlatharta's latest work referred?

He pulled out the book again and read the poem in his stuttering Irish and the line "I am the keeper of the key between these lines..." jumped out at him. What key? Jack had presumed this key to be a key to the void that existed between Irish and English. The new interpretation made sense to Jack. The only likely residence in "this no-mans-land" between railway and canal - apart from rabbit warrens and badger sets - could be a lock-keeper's house. So a poem Jack believed referred to an intellectual or metaphysical "no man's land" was also the place of physical exile to which The OFlatharta had banished himself.

However, as far as the eye could see there were no locks or lock-keepers' houses. Which way to go? Retrace his steps eastwards along the canal. Or keep going west? At this point two young Traveller boys who had been fishing for eels or fresh-water mullet on the canal tow-path climbed up onto the bridge. He'd noticed their caravans tucked away beyond bridge and town as a possible place of sanctuary for the night. Jack was friendly with a family of McCanns who lived in Clondalkin. As all Traveller families knew each other, they might take him in. Then again, if they weren't friendly with this branch of McCanns, they might do him in. Travellers were more than a match for poets when it came to feuding.

> - You're lost Mister.
> - No, I'm not but I'm looking for a man you might know.
> - We might and then again we mightn't.

The older of the two decided to play hard-ball. All Jack's powers of negotiation would be required here.

> - What's his name?

The second lad could not with-hold his innate Traveller curiosity.

> - OFlatharta...Uinsionn OFlatharta. He's a poet.
> - What's that?

Shouted the younger.

The older boy looked at him as if he was stupid.

> - Ballads. It's a fella makes ballads, but leaves the music out.

This didn't make sense to the younger boy: the Travellers were great lovers of music.

- Isn't that right?

The older boy looked at Jack for reassurance.

- Exactly, so do you know where the fellow who writes the ballads but leaves the music out lives?

- Why would we tell you?

- Because The OFlatharta is a great friend of the Travellers.

This was true. As fellow outcasts from so-called civilised society, The OFlatharta had eulogised the Travellers in his poetry.

- Is that right? How comes we never heard of him then?

Jack was getting desperate. The parallel lines of The OFlatharta's poem were now disappearing in the twilight and with them all Jack's hopes of finally having tracked down the poet. Jack decided to cut to the chase.

- Listen lads, The OFlatharta lives in a house on the canal, beside a lock. That's his picture there on the back of this book. East or West? Which is it?

- He must be famous, is he?

- Yes he is?

- Does that mean you're famous?

- No, it doesn't. Now listen can you just tell me?

The older of the two reacted sullenly to Jack's raised voice. Then he looked at Jack's bicycle.

- That's a good bicycle Mister. Did you come all the way from Dublin on that?

Jack regretted not entertaining the boy's interest in fame.

- Yes, and I have to get back there on it as well.

He didn't like the way the conversation was going. He treasured this bike.

- If you're not famous, then you must have a pile of money.

- Nothing could be further from the truth.

- Are you sure?

- Absolutely.

- Well, can I have a go on your bike?

- Can I have a go on your bike?

The little fella piped up in higher octave.

- You can both have a go on it...

Jack was beginning to feel resentful towards the older boy.

- ...when you tell me whether the poet lives that way or that way.

Jack made the mistake of taking his hands off the bike to gesture and the older boy grabbed the bicycle off him and set off down the steep incline of Coon Bridge. In his effort to stop him, Jack tripped over the younger boy who laughed enthusiastically at his brother's swift grab.

- You better stay here.

Jack said sternly, taking the younger boy by the scruff of the neck.

- That is, if you want to have a go on my bike.

XIV

The Serpent Dined

- More wine?

Skiddy leaned over the table, gently brushing Rosa's arm, repressing a belch in appreciation of the feed of spaghetti neapolitana and garlic bread he had just polished off. Not bad for one of these nonsense vegetarian dishes he had often smelled wafting from their living quarters as he set off home to his bed-sit. That the girl could cook opened up another vista of intimate fire-side dinners to come. He noticed her looking at the poised bottle in contemplation.

- We better leave some for Jack. He could be back any minute.

The Comrade was not coming back in a hurry, though Skiddy had to let on. He knew she knew too. Hapless Hermes had obviously fallen hook-line-and-sinker for the task that Skiddy had set him. What a credulous gobshite he was. Ready to believe in any cause that came along. Skiddy repressed a smile as he pictured The Comrade pedalling around the back-roads of The Pale and beyond: he'd spotted his bicycle lamps as he came up the stairs. He'd not be coming back tonight. How he'd love to be there when The OFlatharta opened the letter Skiddy had written him. Skiddy was in no doubt that Jack would find him. He was a persistent fucker, if nothing else.

His own glass was empty, but he didn't want to appear greedy. He decided to share a while in Rosa's concern while rolling a nice thick post-prandial joint. Things were still far too tense. He pulled three cigarette papers in quick succession from their packet and deftly joined them with the aid of a thin line of spittal along the glue. He cracked open a straight and emptied its contents into the patchwork of papers.

- Where did he say he was going?

- To find a poet called The OFlatharta who lives in Meath. Do you know him?

Skiddy had to be careful here. He focused on the task at hand, rolling the unstable structure into an inelegant elongated spliff. He couldn't let on to know much, but always found it hard to suppress his superior knowledge. He eased his tongue along the line of glue and deftly closed his creation.

- Not personally. He's from out west somewhere.

It might seem too neat to speak of his childhood encounters with The OFlatharta on Spiddal Pier which of course were completely fictitious.

However, Skiddy could demonstrate a knowledge of his work. He started to ream off his collections while plugging a card-board roach into the joint.

- Lost Country, Youth Lost, Lost Island. He's got a new collection out.

He noticed how Rosa seemed relieved by Skiddy's verification of the poet's existence.

- According to Jack he's the most important living connection to Martin Meaney?

- I don't know about that...

Skiddy never liked to be seen to agree with Jack, but he needed to soften the put-down. He lit the joint and pulled hard on it. The smoke caught him in the back of the throat. He held his breath for a moment to prevent him spluttering, relaxed, then exhaled.

- There's others would disagree.

- Such as?

- Paddy Jenkins for one.

Rosa seemed interested in the connection. A piece of burning hash fell on the floor and Skiddy quickly stamped on it. Rosa hardly seemed to notice.

- Jack mentioned that Jenkins had asked him to go and find the man.

Before he delivered his next curved ball, Skiddy took the opportunity to fill their glasses.

- That can't be right.

- Why?

- Don't you know the story about Jenkins and The OFlatharta? Rosa shook her head.

- They can't stand each other.

He noticed how Rosa drew from the filled glass as if gasping for air.

- Something to do with The OFlatharta's time in Trinity. Apparently, both of them were up for the same job. It's well known that after writing, Lost Island I think it was, The OFlatharta had been forsaken by The Muse and was ready to try his hand at academic life to sort himself out with a pension. He was believed to be a shoe-in for the job.

He noticed how expectant Rosa now looked so he passed her the joint and she accepted it inexpertly in an absent-minded kind of way.

- Until stories started going around about him and his political sympathies. This was around the time The Troubles started in the North.

- Go on!

- There was no question who put the story around.

- Who?

Rosa was really jumpy now. She pulled on the joint before pouring herself another glass of wine.

- Who do you think? The only other candidate for the job, of course.

Skiddy had to resist mentioning the feud over the woman both men coveted as this might blow his authorship of the Bizniz article now hitting the shelves, but he could not resist an impersonation, that impersonation Jack had so easily fallen for in his crank phone-call to Bewleys.

- Professor Paddy Jenkins.

Skiddy watched as Rosa absorbed this news. He could see the look of jealousy clouding her face. It was not pretty, but in time it would give way to anger and desire, if only out of revenge.

- Then why would he ask Jack to go and find him?

This was no time to spare the girl's feelings.

- Are you sure that's who he's gone to see? Uinsionn OFlatharta is the last person Paddy Jenkins would want at the Memorial Service. Those two hate each other's guts. Is there anyone else out there he might be going to see?

From the look on Rosa's face there clearly was. Skiddy knew exactly who she was thinking of: Kate Keane.

At this point, she left the room without answering. He contemplated following her but decided to sit tight.

Skiddy had already taken a good look around the place when he arrived. It was a comfortable pad, spacious, dried flowers in the window sills, books on the shelves, too many Marxist tracts for his liking, but some good ones all the same which he resisted lifting. This was a cultured household to which he wished to belong. To the sound of crashing pots and pans below he had flicked through The Comrade's recent writings - atrocious - and had even taken a lie down on the bed. How civilised to be able to see the night sky through the sky-light of the attic room. He could do without The Comrade's poetry - in which he appeared to have adopted the persona of some working class Robin Hood - but he now so wanted to take possession of The Comrade's life. Now or never.

He knew somewhere in the back of his mind that in the wooing of the clay he might just lose his wings, but he was getting hard, just at the

121

thought of being in that bed. Had Rosa gone to turn the sheets down? Calm yourself boy. The night is young. He poured himself another glass of wine to distract himself from his fantasies. Don't want to blow your load too soon. Make way Comrade. Remember what Nietzsche said: "What doesn't kill you makes you stronger".

XV

Mister Bizniz

From the height of Coon Bridge the central reservation between railway and canal had not seemed so dense and overgrown. Jack had contemplated walking along the railway line, but a goods train had come hurtling along the narrow single-line cut. He didn't want to risk getting caught down there by another.

The night was clear and already alive with animal movement and moon-shadow. Briars and white-thorn were ripping at his clothes and he had been stung numerous times around the ankles by fresh spring nettles. He stopped for a moment to look back at the village of Coon, its wan street lights almost out of sight. He cursed its tight-lipped people and their outcast population of Travellers alike. He had cherished that bike more than any other possession. He hoped Jenkins and The OFlatharta would appreciate his sacrifice when they finally shook hands in Trinity's Front Square tomorrow.

On realising that Jack was not going to release his little brother, the older boy had returned without bicycle in the company of two older youths. When they asked him what he was doing holding on to the little boy he said he was waiting for his bike to come back; the older boy had taken it without his permission and it was his only means of getting out of there. To his surprise they seemed to believe him. As further explanation he told them he was looking for the poet The OFlatharta at which point one of them said.
- That bollocks that writes the ballads.
- Well, they're poems!
- They're not big on him round here...
Jack couldn't believe it. Finally someone in the vicinity of Coon was prepared to acknowledge the presence of Uinsionn OFlatharta in their midst. The lad's voice picked up.
- ...but he's still a friend of The Travellers.
- I knew it. He lives between the railway and the canal, doesn't he?
- He does.
- Can you just tell me, is it that way or that way?
Jack said pointing East and West for the enth time.
- Don't tell him!

The boy who had taken the bike said. The two youths looked at Jack and then at the boy with disturbing uncertainty. The Travellers always stuck together when it came to dealing with settled people. He would have to up the stakes and make the young boy pay. He addressed the older youths.

- Listen lads, you know I said I'd given your brother there a go on the bike.

- He promised me a go too.

Said the youngest boy who had remained quiet since his release by Jack.

- Well you can keep the bike...
- What make is she?
- Raleigh Racer Ten Speed...
- Class!
- ...if you just tell me which way it is.
- That's not your bike!

The thief yelled.

- That sounds like a fair deal.

The youth had decided where self-interest lay as he turned to the boy and shouted.

- You should have told the man. OFlatharta is a friend of The Travellers.

He continued as he lifted his arm and pointed into the western sky where the fires of the sun were now feint embers in the grey ashes of the day. Jack had lost his bike, but he had taught the thief a lesson in decency.

A new stretch of canal and railway line opened up to him. He examined the way ahead for any sign of habitation, but there was none. Furthermore, the central reservation was proving increasingly difficult to negotiate. There was no turning back now as he beat on into a dense thicket of sally and briars. He imagined it alive with rodents and other wild-life. It hadn't even occurred to him yet what he would say to The OFlatharta when they came face to face, but he was beginning to feel elated at the possibility of completing his mission. The image of that peace-making handshake was the mirage that now drove him on through the darkness. He never once stopped to consider the absurdity of his position: a penniless, bike-less and hopelessly unknown poet beating his way through long abandoned territory in search of a sulking poet who was well able to sort out his own differences. And yet he felt a peace in himself, as if he was close to some major discovery of his life. Was this to be his destiny? Diplomacy? The world and all ills could open up to him in this moment and he would happily surrender himself.

Which it did. He should have been watching where he was going when he lost his footing and tumbled into a deep drainage ditch, a fall only partly cushioned by a bed of leaves and rotting winter debris. As he lay there in the silence, listening to his own breath, the sound of clackety clack began to grow. Clambering out of the ditch, he rose to a vantage point at the edge of the thicket as the last train from Sligo came careening along the line drowning out all other sound, the lights from its gloomy carriages of statuesque passengers illuminating the rail corridor and the thicket about him and what Jack thought was a steep slated roof peeking out of the trees. A badger burst its cover in terror, at the passing train, knocking Jack to his feet again. He couldn't help emitting a cry of pain and shock.

As he clambered up the ditch, the narrow woodland was returning to an eerie silence. In that growing silence he heard a whisper, but a distinct whisper. It was the sound of falling water. He beat on through nature's debris, the sound of falling water resonant off lock walls and the crucible of trees. And there it was: the building he thought imagined in spilt train light, was yielding its own low electric light. In that symphony of water-flow and bird call he heard the strains of ORíada's Mise Éire. Over this the sound of mournful chanting. Someone was at home.

The thicket gave way to a garden that ran between the borders of railway and canal. Jack could barely make out the figures of statues and other garden ornaments amidst the array of shrubs and bushes. At the end of the lawn, a flight of stairs rose to a modest stone house, made imposing by its siting on the upper deck of the lock. This was like a druid's castle. It was a druid's castle. The chanting had ceased and the radio was now being re-tuned to the Radio Éireann shipping forecast. Why anyone living in land-locked Coon Parish would be interested in conditions at sea was beyond him. Jack focused on the encounter to come and on how he would introduce himself to The OFlatharta: "Member of the Dublin Poetry Collective"? "Fellow disciple of Martin Meaney"? No he couldn't attempt to put himself on the same rung as the man he was about to meet. What about? "Uinsionn OFlatharta, you are the most important living link to Meaney, please bury the hatchet and come to the Memorial Service". Jack approached the steps and was about to start his ascent when a voice from above stopped him in his tracks.

125

- What do you want?

The deliberate diction denoted the native Irish speaker still bristling with the English.

- Tá mé ag lorg An tUasal Uinsionn OFlatharta.

Jack replied in his best Irish. Not good enough for the addressee who promptly replied in English.

- Who sent you?

Still the same deliberate and monotonal delivery. Jack could barely make out the towering figure of a man standing on the terrace.

- I have a message from Professor Patrick Jenkins of Trinity College for An tUasal Uinsionn OFlathartha.

- Why would that man want to send a message to Uinsionn OFlatharta?

Jack remembered the feud and thought he should appeal to the poet's sense of the common good. After all, he was the most important living connection to Meaney.

- We all want to honour Martin Meaney.

Presuming the silence implied a yielding on the part of the venerable poet, Jack decided to push home with his best shot.

- An tUasal Uinsionn OFlatharta, you are the most important living connection to Martin Meaney.

- He's a liar!

His opening démarche had fallen on deaf ears. The years had obviously not softened the OFlatharta's view of the feud. This was going to be difficult.

- Well I would have certain ideological differences with the man in question...

- Who would not?

- ... but I'm sure he means well.

Silence.

- And you are?

Jack always felt embarrassed talking about himself with one so talented and revered as The OFlatharta.

- We're a group of poets...

- We?

The OFlatharta scanned his garden for any poets who might be concealed there.

- I asked who you are?

- It doesn't matter who I am.

- Yes it does. You are on my property.

He had forgotten how property-conscious the Conamara people were. Sarcastic too.

- We're based in the old Hi Brasil on Parnell Square.
- The Hi Brasil. The nights we had.
- You know it?
- You didn't answer my question. "It doesn't matter who I am".
The OFlatharta liked the comfort of his sarcasm.
- What kind of poet would say such a thing?
Jack decided to press on.
- We've been working with Paddy Jenkins...
The OFlatharta raised his hand to cease any further explanation.
- I know who you are.
- You do?
- Yes, I heard you were looking for me. Why so coy?
Jack seemed relieved. Word had obviously reached him from the village of Coon.
- Good, because nobody seemed to know where to find you.
- It is always good to keep your public guessing, Jack Lennon.
How had he learned his name?
- You're certainly elusive, if you don't mind me saying so.
- You don't stand still yourself, it appears.
Jack didn't know what to make of this. The OFlatharta was now observing the star-lit sky while taking a deep breath of the damp night air. His mood appeared to shift as he smelt the wind.
- Beidh sé ag seoltóireacht anocht.
The shipping forecast was now making some sense to Jack. The gale warning on the Irish Sea had been lifted. Meaney would soon be embarking on the final leg of his journey from Holyhead under the watch of the clearing heavens. As he followed OFlatharta up the steps he was about to enquire of these "nights" in the Hi Brasil and if they had been spent in the company of Martin Meaney when he remembered the envelope that Jenkins had entrusted to him. He produced it from his canvas bag and presented it to The OFlatharta who in turn looked at it with suspicion.
- Did he give you any money for me?
Jack shrugged his shoulders and looked at the envelope.
- It is a tradition where I come from that when you wrong a man you pay him compensation.
The OFlatharta appeared to be lost in thoughts of resentment for the sender, oblivious to the phone ringing in the house above them. Perhaps confirmation of Meaney's despatch by the Druids of Anglesea was at hand. The old man took off into the house, ushering Jack into the kitchen with a rough wave of the hand.
- Tar isteach!

Jack dutifully followed. The interior of the house had none of the imposing feel of the exterior. Not the hermit's retreat he had imagined. Its tidiness reminded Jack of the poet's past as a book-keeper in the English Civil Service. The kitchen-cum-library had a cocoon-like feel to it. It felt more like the cabin of a sea-faring boat.

Jack saw that the letter from Jenkins lay unopened on the table. As he studied it for the first time, he thought he noticed a familiar flourish to the hand-writing. He could hear The OFlatharta talking lowly into the phone, uttering the odd gruff affirmation in response to what he was being told, then silence. Suddenly, the receiver was slammed onto the cradle. Bad news. Meaney couldn't be even more dead than he already was. Perhaps the Brits had decided to bury him in the desolation of Anglesea. Jack could feel the hairs rise on the back of his neck as the angry poet entered the room, the phone slam still resonating. OFlatharta circled the table, lifting the letter and swiftly opening it.

    - Bad news about Meaney?
    - You've been a busy man whoever you are.
    - My name is Jack, Jack Lennon.
    - Maybe we should call you Mister Bizniz?
    - Why would you do that?
    - How much did they pay you to commit idle pillow talk to print?

The man was obsessed with money.

    - Nothing.
    - Let's see what kind of a brass neck you have in the hands of The OFlatharta.

With that The OFlatharta grabbed him round the neck and held him firmly.

    - Did Jenkins put you up to that too?
    - No one put me up to anything.

Jack was already short of breath.

    - Jenkins' little messenger.

All Jack could do was shake his head.

    - Did he give you this?

Letter and envelope were stuffed into his face.

    - Not personally!
    - "Not personally".

He mocked Jack's attempts to maintain a sense of perspective.

    - Then who gave it to you?
    - The Porters.
    - And who gave it to The Porters?

The older man imitated Jack again. Jack was beginning to see how The OFlatharta had alienated so many people over the years. He had a violent temper and a biting sarcasm.

- Jenkins, I suppose.

- You suppose? Well what is this supposed to mean?

The OFlatharta pulled Jack forward by the neck, until his nose pressed against the bonded sheet of Trinity headed-paper. Jack could now easily read the one word scrawled across the page.

- "Gotcha!"

The man now lifted the envelope with the other hand and shoved it into Jack's face.

- Now do you see that?

Jack studied the scrawling of OFlatharta's name on the envelope. Something wasn't right about it.

- Spell OFlatharta!

With his ailing breath Jack dutifully spelt the poet's surname remembered from the jacket of Between The Lines/Idir Na Línta.

- Correct! OFlatharta spelt with only the one 'T' aspirated.

The spray from the old sea dog's storm was now aspirating Jack's face, but he was too weakened to move. He was losing consciousness.

- Now, Patrick Jenkins may be a liar, a thief and a bad poet, but one thing he is not is illiterate. Explain, Mister Bizniz!

Jack could only think of one word with which to explain. He looked directly at the poet with all the sincerity he could muster. The word came out more as a plaintive question than a statement of fact, though he was in no doubt who had set him up so brilliantly.

- Skiddy!

XVI
The Witch and The Serpent

Rosa had always considered herself the quintessential Virgo. Virgo intacto. Organised, self-contained, communicative and, above all, faithful. Now she was preparing to commit an infidelity with the most untrustworthy person she had ever met. She had always presumed she would be the first to commit an infidelity. Now Jack with his butter wouldn't melt in his mouth, holier-than-thou-man-with-a-mission superiority was at it with Kate Keane. What an elaborate and fanciful deceiver he was. If he had just told her that he had needed time to consider their relationship she would have gone along with his need for space. Through his actions he had left the door wide open for the Serpent to slip through. Now she understood why. So he could be with her. The image of Kate Keane and Jack doing it together in some ditch in County Meath invaded her thoughts. She needed to banish them. The sound of movement from the hall distracted her. This was not the hermaphrodite coming to call. The serpent had supplanted the hermaphrodite. She looked at her pale face in the bathroom mirror and reached into the cabinet for her diaphragm.

By the time she entered the bedroom what she saw was not Skiddy's pink Corrib salmon nakedness sprawled across her bed, glass of wine in one hand, a newly rolled joint in the other, but the shape of the serpent circling, preparing to bring her pleasures denied by another. She approached the serpent with a look of cold recognition and started to strip. This was not their first encounter, she remembered.

Was he psychic enough to have received that first invitation? She climbed on the bed and straddled him. His torso rose up to meet her. She turned her head to avoid his overeager kiss and he licked her ear instead. She turned her head again and he latched onto the other ear, then bit it. She pulled away and eyed him, unwilling to let him leave his mark. Responding to the struggle, he thrust at her. She felt his sex hardening at the touch of hers. Not yet. She couldn't feel him hard enough yet to put him in. One stroke of her sex on his was enough to remedy that, but not so fast. This snake seemed far too eager to share his venom. He seemed to accept her invitation to play and let his hand stray to her behind. She thrust forward again, but he seemed transfixed, distracted by something. Unable to continue the initiative he started to emit a short choked "Jesus". She decided this was it and started to thrust even harder against him. "No" he seemed to say in his riveted state, eyes still fixed on the sky-light. "Yes" she replied more to herself now as she reached down with her hand to fill the space his deflating penis had abandoned. Was that it? What was the distraction? She closed her eyes oblivious to his contorted state and imagined the hermaphrodite coming to embrace her cold back. Throwing her head back, she felt its arms embrace her: the twins whispering his name in either ear. The sound of Jack's name appeared to fill the room as if from another's voice. The white light was beginning to come out of the darkness, the warm hands of the hermaphrodite kneading her on.

- Oh Jack!

She heard herself say. That felt better. She repeated his name again, half in sorrow, half in pleasure; his name echoed around the house as she called out to him as if each cavernous room of the abandoned hotel was calling back to her in a chorus. Eyes closed, she felt the cry rise in her throat. In the warm embrace of the hermaphrodite Rosa came with an involuntary jerk of her body.

- Jack!

When she finally opened her eyes to look at the sky-light she could feel the light of the full-moon on her face. Was that what had jinxed Skiddy? The phone was ringing in the hall but she was not only unable to move but unable to speak. Jack's name still echoed through the building as if another had taken up the call. Someone else had. All she could hear was a spooked Skiddy saying with what sounded like a dying breath.

- Whathefuckwasthat? Whathefuckwasthat?

It occurred to Rosa that Skiddy had obviously never heard a woman come before.

Whathefuckwasthat? Whathefuckwasthat? That was weird, but this was even more so. That voice still calling Jack's name was all too familiar. Was it in the building? Was it outside the building. Rosa had vacated the bed, presumably to tidy up or out of some sudden bout of shyness or regret.

Still waters run deep. The Comrade had a much more interesting existence than Skiddy could have imagined behind that butter wouldn't melt in his mouth christian charity marxist facade. And Skiddy might fit well into his place, even if Rosa had to pretend it was Jack she was having it off with. He'd obviously really done it for the dame the way she had gone crazy for it. He found himself growing hard at the memory. Delay yourself boy. She'd be back soon enough. What a show she had put on, taking over the reins for the sprint home when he had dropped them in his distraction at the face staring at him through the sky-light. He remembered that face from a week before, hustling him for a fag outside the Rotunda as he parleyed with Paddy Jenkins. Obviously some hobo of the roof-tops. He would see to him if he showed his face again.

Lying in this bed was his reward for perseverance and forbearance. Forbearance of The Comrade's awful auld clap-trap about collective action. No collective action here comrade, just me and her. Perseverance, despite Rosa's evasion over recent weeks. Now he'd bedded her would he lose her as his muse? At least before bedding her he'd got some work done and now he was in prime position to claim the Meaney Medal & Money.

If he won he'd take her on a weekend to Galway where he could parade her with his medal about the place, reciting his winning poem in every watering hole in the damn town. But in Galway he'd have to introduce her to his mother. He didn't think he was ready for that. Fuck Galway. He'd take her to Paris and they could blow the whole shagging thousand pounds. They'd shack up in a hotel in Montmartre and blow each others brains out with sex and booze and when the craziness had passed, they'd stalk the Boulevard Montparnasse for sightings of the aged Beckett and they could all sit in a boulevard café and bitch about Jenkins.

What if he got her up the pole? Skiddy would cherish that child of passion, marry the wench and they'd have a whole brood of gasurs. Little poets one and all. He'd write poetry in the day-time and he could go to the pub at night while she tended house and reared the youngsters. She seemed like the open-minded sort so she would understand if he kept one foot on the wild-side. After all, she might get stability from The Comrade, but she clearly wasn't getting enough of IT. Guilty? No. This was the way it had to be. This world couldn't work if people just stood back all the time. No no. You first. No, you, I insist that you have what I really want but I'm just too much of a Christian to say I want it. The kind of repressive behaviour that gave you cancer.

He contemplated re-lighting the joint, but decided instead to find out where she'd got to, just in case she'd succumbed to a bout of the guilts. He grabbed a dressing gown and set off to explore the lower regions of the house.

Rosa was in the kitchen and it was clear she was not alone.

- I'm sorry love, but it's best you know.

- I thought when he was working nights he was still here in the building, but keeping another flat going. Where did you say you spent the night together?

- Rathmines. It's nothing as beautiful as what you have here. To be honest, I wouldn't have come, but there are others who are more angry with him than I have a right to be.

Skiddy peeked through the kitchen door. The first thing that caught his eye was the cover of Bizniz magazine: a photomontage of Jenkins and OFlatharta on the front having their heads hopped together by the Taoiseach. The next thing he saw was the arm of a familiar-looking fur-coat reaching out to comfort Rosa. Mrs. Thatcher. The phone was ringing in the hall again.

- Do you want to get that?

Brenda Barron enquired of Rosa.

- I can't speak to him now.

Time for Skiddy to get the fuck out of there. But his jacket was there in the kitchen and his clothes were upstairs. Shit. He couldn't waste any time. He was not in the mood for another tête à tête with Mrs. Thatcher.

XVII
A Lesson in Loss

Jack listened to their phone ring out. He was relieved to find nobody at home. Rosa had obviously done the wise thing and left the house for the night. Returning to the kitchen, he found The OFlatharta much calmed from the assault. Perhaps he was relieved that his feud with Jenkins was still intact and being cherished by the next generation. He had really only calmed down after he spoke by phone to one of his people who gave him a physical description of the young man who had posed as Jack at the Arts and Literary. Jack had then verified the identity of the impostor.

A plate of food had been produced and a glass of wine. Not for the first time in his life, Jack felt in the wrong place at the wrong time. The OFlatharta noticed his reticence and ordered him to sit, which Jack obediently did. The OFlatharta resumed his rehearsal for tomorrow's oration after the interruption of Jack's arrival. With a couple of notes added to the text, The OFlatharta seemed pleased enough to resume his conversation with Jack.

- Why would this Skiddy fella want to send you on a wild goose chase like this?
- He disapproves of my politics.
- Which are?
- I believe that poets should be working together against the forces of ignorance and oppression. Brits out of the north and then let's deal with the gangsters who run this corrupt little state of ours.
- And how would you propose to do that?
- Consciousness raising. The creation of a new Irish man and woman.
- And you'll be leading the consciousness-raising?
- There won't be any leaders, but I'm prepared to do my bit.
- This sounds like a very chaotic revolution. I'm not sure I want to be a part of it. It might give us poets an even worse reputation for impracticality than we already have.
- Well you can sit back and take the benefits, Mr OFlatharta. You've already done your bit.
- Thank you!
Silence descended as Jack wolfed his vittels. The OFlatharta looked like he was considering his proposal.

- Did it occur to you that the average Irish man and woman might like things the way they are?

- They think they like things that way because that's all they know. When the people's heads aren't so full of football and shopping and they have the facts...

- Facts? What in the name of God does poetry have to do with the facts?

- Truth.

Jack sounded very sure of himself.

- If truth is based on facts I dread to see the poetry your revolution will produce. Without decent poetry, your revolution is destined to fail.

Jack was trying to work out what else truth could be based upon. The OFlatharta's thesis was clearly based on the necessity of his art and therefore hardly empirical. Jack realised he had got The OFlatharta onto his favourite theme of failure and loss and decided to hold fire. The next question took him by surprise.

- Have you ever lost anything, boy?

- I've gained more than I have lost.

- That's not what I asked you.

- Well the Travellers just took my bicycle at Coon Bridge, but I'd have had to leave it there anyway...

- Never lost someone?

- Like who?

- A loved one.

- Well everybody's lost somebody sometime.

The OFlatharta examined him closely, sensing his vulnerability.

- You are not everybody. Éist dom! Uinsionn OFlatharta is an expert in loss and I detect that you have lost some body.

Jack wondered if The OFlatharta thought of himself as one of these Shamans that Rosa sometimes spoke about. As if reading his mind, The OFlatharta changed the subject.

- So, do you have a girl?

Jack was slow to answer.

- Or maybe you're into the men?

- That's very open minded of you.

- Thank you, but you didn't answer my question.

- Rosa! Rosa is her name.

He wondered how she was managing with him away.

- Rosa, a beautiful name.

- She's a bit annoyed at me for coming out here.

- You forsook her for me, I'm honoured. Did you ever tell Rosa that you loved her?

Jack saw a piece of foam forming at the edge of the man's mouth.

- Did you?

He thought he should attempt an answer.

- What's love? It's such an abstract...

He could see the red patch grow on The OFlatharta's neck under tufts of white hair.

- What is love?

The man stared into Jack's face, eye-ball to eye-ball.

- Love is Truth!

The OFlatharta nearly washed him overboard with the force of his spray. Then under his breath he delivered his crushing verdict.

· - You will lose her for sure.

Well that was his thesis for everything. Loss. Lost Country, Youth Lost, Lost Island, Lost Rosa. However, he was presenting Jack with an eventuality he had not fully considered. Life without Rosa. Where would his revolution be without her? He had managed well before Rosa and he would manage when she was gone, the way he had managed after his parents' death. The thought began to upset him as much as the anger being visited on him by the great OFlatharta. It might have been the food and the wine on his empty stomach, but suddenly he felt fevered, his whole body in a sweat.

- I better be going, Mister OFlatharta.

- You will stay the night. I don't wish to be fishing you from the canal in the morning.

The OFlatharta said definitively.

- No really, you needn't!

- I insist!

Jack relented under order.

- But you must assure me of one thing.

Jack waited expectantly,

- That when you rise to relieve yourself in the night, on no account avail of the outdoors.

- You have my word.

- There has been many a night-time meanderer and philanderer nearly perish on lock or line.

Jack saw the sense of this and assured him that he had a good bladder and always slept through the night.

XVIII
Winged Ariadne

Getting to know the great stage actress Brenda Barron would have been an honour if she wasn't still preoccupied with the image of Jack having sex with this woman the same age as his deceased mother. If this was how he was dealing with this loss, he needed help. Brenda Barron seemed to think so too: if Jack had indeed gone to see the OFlatharta as he had told Rosa, perhaps to gain further information on behalf of Bizniz, word of Bizniz might have reached The OFlatharta ahead of his arrival. The man it seemed had an unfathomable temper which was why she couldn't bring herself to phone on Rosa's behalf. What's more she no longer had his number as The OFlatharta who was obsessed with his privacy regularly changed it and there were few people who would give her the number after her indiscretions.

Rosa presumed Jack had gone to be with Kate Keane, but now she didn't know what to believe. Perhaps Skiddy who appeared to have made such a rapid departure after their triste had been goading her into believing this for his own ends. She asked Brenda where The OFlatharta lived and the answer instilled more terror in her than the image of Jack lying in the arms of Kate Keane.
- In a most beautiful cottage by the canal.
Brenda said this with a wistfulness for lost love.
- Canal? Which canal?
Brenda promptly volunteered the co-ordinates. This all made sense to Rosa. Finally he had gone looking for them. He should have just gone to the memorial service to make his piece with their passing.
- Tell me one thing about your time with Jack. Did he sleepwalk for you too Brenda?
Brenda blushed at being reminded of these events.
- To be honest darling, we were so pissed.
Rosa repressed her feelings of disdain for her unexpected visitor and preferred to remember her awesome Pegeen Mike. Brenda Barron was a masterful exponent of the iconic female roles.
- We have to go there.
Rosa insisted.
- I can't.
Rosa looked at her with that look that could halt a runaway train.
- You must.
Brenda Barron would be directed.

Rosa had never been in an E-Type Jag before. Brenda could sense Rosa's admiration of the car and for her driving.

    - My little present to myself from my soap days.

They followed the North Circular Road, branching off across The Phoenix Park and took the back-roads to Lucan by the Strawberry Beds to avoid the Guards. Maynooth was soon behind them. Rosa's hunch about Brenda's past relationship with The OFlatharta was justified. She clearly knew all the backroads from Maynooth to the village of Coon and when the E-Type Jag accelerated up the steep incline of Coon Bridge towards the star-lit sky, it felt like they might jump the moon as the car left the surface of the road for what seemed like seconds before landing short of a hair-pin bend, which Brenda rounded with a shift of the gears and a screech of brakes. It was now past midnight and as Jack had been on the go all day after last night's infidelities with her chauffeur, he would soon be sleeping and once he was asleep he was a danger to himself. This was no time for safety measures.

XIX
Lost and Found

Jack's eyes flew open. He had no idea where he was. All he knew was this familiar dream. A dream of water. The water of a canal at night, somewhere peaceful in the Irish countryside. The sound of falling water calling him to pee. His body sweating profusely. He had to throw off these clothes. The lot. He had to go. Could he interrupt this dream, this dream he repeatedly entertained? He could hear their car. Imagined it. They weren't watching the road ahead like they should have been. They were arguing about something. He couldn't hear what they were arguing about. Never seemed to matter as long as they could disagree. This was the game in which they were locked. Just stop arguing he heard himself say. Can't everyone just agree, for once? But they were ignoring him. He would do anything for them just to stop, but it was too late. He could hear the sound of their car approaching now. The car was hurtling at speed through the silence of the night. They'd missed the signs telling them not to go there. They were heading up a dead end. They were heading from earth to water. Sun and moon now in the sky. Now in the grip of the crisp outdoors the sound of water called him to relieve himself. He could see the lights of the car from the vantage of the lock gate. He could hear the sound of their argument above the roar of the engine. Their arguments were the narrative of his childhood. You said this and I said that. The sun and moon of the headlights of an oncoming car blinding him over the angry roar. As he watched from the lock gate he heard the screech of brakes and the awful grinding of tyres on gravel. The futility of this action as the momentum of car and engine propelled them forward into the arms of the deep lock. The machine cracked against the far wall of the lock and crumpled as far as the engine head, pistons now driving hot liquid and gases into the canal waters. Straddling the lock, the vehicle remained suspended for what seemed like an age. Against the windscreen Jack could see the stricken faces of his parents.

He approached the canal lock, naked as the day he was born, his sun and moon in peril. Take me with you he asked as the engine began to scrape violently down the walls of the lock. They weren't listening to him. They were looking at each other. They weren't reaching out for him. They were reaching out for each other. Save yourself, he thought he heard a voice say. Not them. Let them take each other down.

Standing on the precipice he watched the car slide into the dark waters and submerge, headlights illuminating the dark recesses of the lock, leaving him in the dark. Denied their heat he felt himself growing cold in the dark. Take me back to your heat, dear sun and moon. To an accompaniment of falling water and the violent blast from pockets of air hitting the surface, he took one step forward ready to plunge into the canal to save his drowning parents. This was his mission in life: to reverse the irreversible, to save the un-saveable, to win the un-winnable. Preparing to leap forward into the dark he felt the warmth of an arm catching him around the waist. He looked around into the face of his assailant. The face of a young woman. He fought to free himself so he could complete his rescue mission. The woman restrained him further. Was this his parents' persecutor? Hardly. Had she set this trap for his parents? His assailant raised her hand and slapped him firmly across the face. Restrained, he found himself staring into the empty lock, the car completely submerged now, its lights fading into the cold dark waters. He turned to look at the face of the woman still restraining him and thought he recognised her as Rosa, the young woman with whom he shared his life.

Jack looked down at his naked trembling body. Rosa held him close, spooked by the near tragedy she had just witnessed. From the kitchen-door The OFlatharta came to survey the scene.

- I take it you have found what you were looking for, Mister No Name.

XX

She Is The She of It

Jack woke to the sound of a passing goods train. Its departure left only the sound of a thrush's song and falling water. What a sound sleep he had enjoyed. For a moment he needed to orientate himself. He was lying on the sailor's cot-bed in the kitchen of poet and expert in loss Uinsionn OFlatharta. He turned and looked over his shoulder into the face of Rosa who was sitting at the kitchen table watching him. His voice revealed none of the surprise he felt.

- Rosa!

He was about to ask her what she was doing there when the door opened and The OFlatharta entered with a heap of fresh eggs cradled in his arms.

- Your kit is at the end of the bed, amadán.

Jack only realised that he was naked. The OFlatharta chortled to himself as the lard hit the pan.

- It was some show. You were in the possession of the dead.

Jack looked confused. Rosa only then spoke.

- You were sleepwalking Jack.

- Why didn't you answer the question?

The OFlatharta persisted.

- What question?

- I asked you if you had lost some body and you didn't answer. Whoever it was died out there again last night.

Rosa looked at The OFlatharta to get him to lay off. Jack sat up in the bed clutching the blanket to him.

- OFlatharta is an expert in loss, Rosa.

- Yes, we've been talking.

- I remember the crash. They'd been in The Western Grill for a meal I believe.

The OFlatharta scalded the tea-pot in ceremonial fashion, then something occurred to him.

- They were estranged, weren't they?

- Yes they were!

- So why did they go together?

Jack shrugged his shoulders. He could see The OFlatharta take this in. Here was an epic tale of loss and absence.

- Do you think they meant to drive into the canal?

- No. They were probably having an argument.

- But they loved each other?
Jack thought about this. This had always been difficult for him to see. They often appeared to him more as enemies engaged in mortal combat. But this indeed was a perverse kind of love.

- I suppose they did. They just didn't want anyone to know it. He looked at Rosa as he said this. He hoped she might identify his regret at his own earlier evasions of the L-word. Rosa gave him a reassuring pat on the hand. When he went to take hers she drew away and vacated the kitchen to join Brenda who was smoking in the open-air. He still hadn't worked out how she had ended up here.

- And this is why you have so little time for love, Mister Hermaphrodite?
The OFlatharta was starting to serve out the breakfast.

- Mister what?

- Deny if you like, but I saw IT with my own two eyes.

- Aithníonn ciaróg ciaróg eile.

-Takes one to know one?
Jack was no wiser.

- Do you know another thing?
He said with a nod towards the door that Rosa had exited.

- She is the she of IT.

They ate breakfast and talked, OFlatharta keeping half an ear to the radio for weather reports and anything that might hinder the arrival at port of Martin Meaney. The OFlatharta was in a good mood and had clearly forgiven Brenda for whatever indiscretion she had leaked to Bizniz and Brenda had been relieved that the young man she had slept with the night before was not Jack. Soon all four were speeding towards the city in Brenda's Jag, stopping off at the Travellers' site for the OFlatharta to negotiate the release of Jack's bike.

XXI
The Scaffolder Falls

Dún Laoghaire Pier felt far from funereal. Not since the visit of King George had the waterfront seen such regalia. The imminent arrival of the remains of Martin Meaney had brought every flag-waving Kilkenny man and woman in the capital to the dock; the world of poetry was there in all its shambolic state; not to mention every left-wing sect, the sellers of Trouble – The Relaunch and Socialist Worker staring each other down in their quest for new members. Despite Meaney's professed socialism, the occasion did not appear to her as an appropriate recruiting ground and this was confirmed by the indifference with which the soul-seekers were met. Resolute in their quest, they barely seemed to mind.

Rosa had declined the offer of a lift all the way to the boat and had instead made her excuses to go home and tidy up the mess she had left the night before: the dinner plates, the wine bottles, not to mention Skiddy's clothes. She now understood why he had beat such a hasty retreat in her dressing gown. Brenda's description of the young man who had posed as Jack fitted perfectly. She couldn't dislike him for it. He had only extracted from his female prey what they were prepared to give. What's more, his misleading Jack had inadvertently set him on a necessary if perilous collision course with his grief. What troubled her more was the postman's knock that followed her entrance to No 105 and the registered letter for which she signed on Jack's behalf. Identifying the sender as the Hanley and Slaughter Property Management Company, she could not resist opening and reading it. "Dear Mister Lennon, Your refusal to meet with us to discuss the future management of 105, Parnell Square has left us with no other option than to terminate your position as caretaker of our premises. We advise you to make alternative accommodation arrangements and to vacate the premises forthwith..."

Their home, their life together, revolved so much around this house. These brief lines said so much, not just about the heartlessness of Hanley and Slaughter Property Management, but about Jack's intentions. By not attending the meeting the previous afternoon while pursuing an absurd quest, he had demonstrated his ability to spread his wings and to let his fellow poets make their own way in the world. He had chosen poetry over the trappings of poetry. All he now needed to be completely free was to get this Terry Crowe guy off his back. This required money. No wonder he was looking anxious in the crowd. He looked drawn from the cycle back from County Meath to which Brenda Barron had condemned him, fearful that his bike might scratch the roof of her car. The announcement of the winner of the Martin Meaney Memorial Medal with its prize of 1000 pounds was about to be made.

As she made her way through the respectful mourners, she took in the pungent scents of churned up sea water and burning engine fuel from the Mail Boat now edging closer to the dock. On a hastily mounted PA System she could hear the voice of Paddy Jenkins detailing the arrangements for the Memorial Service to be held in Trinity. Seats only for those who had reserved. She had seen Skiddy skulking on the roadway above the dock, presumably allowing himself the option of a hasty retreat, but obviously curious to hear the results of the Poetry Competition, the poem for which he had shown her the previous evening. It was quite impressive. She had not told him about her own entry because she had no expectation of winning. She would speak to Skiddy again about what had happened between them. Now, she needed to find Jack to give him the news of their imminent eviction. How would he take it?

She located Jack standing with Kate Keane and the other poets. They were all waiting for the conclusion of Jenkins' instructions when he would announce the winner of the inaugual Martin Meaney Memorial Medal, not to mention the money which Jenkins now made clear to the audience had been bequeathed by the dead poet for this specific purpose. This latter detail had moved the majority of the mourners from indifference to Jenkin's announcements to one of hushed silence. Jenkins now cleared his throat and attention was momentarily drawn from the ship now bearing Martin Meaney's remains to the audience itself. Rosa handed Jack the registered letter. He saw the look of concern on her face and started to open the letter.

A polite round of applause followed the announcement of the competition runner-up. Jack barely seemed to react, more absorbed in the letter he was about to read. Jenkins continued with his announcement while Jack read the letter.
    - The winner of the Inaugural Martin Meaney Memorial Medal is Rosa Nugent.

144

The crowd broke into gentle applause. A look of shock crossed Jack's face. The members of the Poetry Collective who were gathered together in the shadow of the harbour wall looked at each other askance. Jack was now shaking his head. Was it the contents of the letter or what had just been announced? As the applause ebbed away, he closed up the letter. Rosa's eyes scanned the audience of fellow poets. On the balcony above her she could see Skiddy glaring at her. He was shaking his head like she just robbed him of his birthright. Rosa looked back at Jack. Jack still looked askance, shaking his head. Was it her win or the contents of the letter to which he was responding. He looked up from the letter.

      - Rosa, I didn't know.

      - You didn't know what, Jack?

      - I didn't know you were a poet.

      - There's a lot you don't know about me.

He seemed to catch the hint of a confession in her voice and turned to look at the object of her fleeting glance over his shoulder. In that moment, all three, Jack, Skiddy and Rosa were looking from one to the other, not knowing where else to look until the ship's horn beckoned them to attention. Silence descended on the throng, but for the screech of hydraulics from the ship's bow. She noticed that Jack still gazed at her as if seeing her with new eyes. He really seemed happy for her in a way that Skiddy clearly wasn't.

      - What's the poem about Rosa?

      - Jack, two things. Never ask a woman her age or a poet the meaning of their work.

      - It's just I can't wait to hear it.

      - You will.

The ship's bow began to rise. Expecting the habitual traffic of cars and lorries to line off in impatient search for their final destination, indifferent to their celebrated cargo, the audience were in fact presented with the gaping jaws of the ship's empty hold. There were clearly a select few in the know as at that moment there was a movement in the crowd above as the slamming doors of a large state car announced the arrival of someone important. There was a stirring on the mirador above the dock that had been cordoned off for family and dignitaries. Rosa identified the diminutive figure of the Taoiseach edging to the front with solemn regal nods to the family of the deceased. The sound of a lone piper emanating from the bowels of the ship called all to attention. They watched in sadness and in wonder as the ship that had spirited so many abroad in this disastrous decade and in earlier decades was preparing to deliver back the self-exiled bones of Martin Meaney.

The Piper stepped from the dimness of the ship into the light of day and behind him, flanked by four crewmen of the MV Patricia, appeared the coffin of Martin Meaney draped in the black and amber of his native Kilkenny and propelled by a fellow miner from the Castlecomer Colliery in the bent "hurrier" stance that had earned Meaney his life-long stoop. As if in deference to his most famous of works, his 1966 memoir "...Born Astride the Gangway", the party halted in that space between ship and shore, allowing complete silence to reign.

At Trinity Rosa told Jack she needed to get her thoughts together before her time came to stand up and recite her winning poem. Outside the gates of Trinity she turned right and headed towards the river. She noticed how spring had put colour into the faces of the people as they waited for their buses or went about their business.

Rosa was walking, not quite aimlessly, reflecting on how she had come to this pass. It was hardly fair that she had won the prize while betraying Jack. But then the two events were not connected or maybe they were. It was the absence he had created in her that had led her to fill it with poetry. It was jealousy over another that had pushed her to betrayal. Yes, she had hinted at a confession, but that was as far as she would go and after all she had made good when she realised her mistake and had acted to avert danger. She would have to learn to nurture that sense of absence he created in her. She would make life better for them first of all by paying off Terry Crowe with the prize-money and then find somewhere new for them to live. She could see their life together in poetry. It wouldn't be easy, but it was definitely a life.

As she walked across O'Connell Bridge from south to north she observed how the north quay was still lower than the south. Jack would have found some social symbolism in that fact. To her in her reflective state it was merely a curious fact. However, it occurred to her that it was one of those quirks that kept the two halves of the city at odds with itself in its age-old psychic conversation with itself.

The city was changing. The coal that caused smog had been outlawed and in the clearing skies cranes were beginning to overhang the city's magnificent church spires. Perhaps the organisers of the city's Millennium celebrations were not just feeding off a mythical past, but were heralding the city's re-invention. Whether this city could nurture their lives anymore she was unsure. Their love had been nurtured in a time of decline, had blossomed in adversity. Now that the place appeared resurgent would they thrive. Could poetry survive in this new culture-as-business revival. She could only hope that poetry would have its place in the plan and that when the city gazed back into the black pool it would not only seek to see its reflection but also what lay beyond. The city had inspired poetry and poetry had played its part in the making of the city. A city needed to dream as a poet dreamed. Not to feed off its past or its dreams of futures past, but to dream its new life.

She still had time to spare as she turned back on her path. Before she spoke with Jack, she needed to clear something up. She had seen him skulking down Poolbeg Street minutes before and this could only mean one thing. She pushed open the door of Mulligans, checked front and back and was on her way out feeling a bit confused when she heard his voice pull her back.

       - You better make that two, barman.

Rosa turned and found Stephen Kieran Dee staring out at her.

       - Looking for someone?

       - Well, you did leave in a hurry the last time we met.

       - I suppose congratulations are in order.

       - Not if you don't want to offer them.

He raised the pint in her direction.

       - Why wouldn't I? You've clearly got what it takes. Good luck.

She considered this as a compliment.

       - And what about you?

       - Poetry is a mugs game. My talents lie elsewhere.

       - You certainly know how to raise a storm.

       - I take that as a compliment.

       - Does this mean you are leaving poetry?

Skiddy nodded his head.

       - We'll miss the excitement.

       - We?

       - Of course. Jack needs you as much as I need you. Look how much you needed him! Until last night I thought it was him you really wanted.

Skiddy pondered this for a moment. He had indeed spent as much time thinking about Jack as Rosa.

- Maybe. I take it from your poem that he is the he and you are the she of it?

Rosa took a sip of her pint and nodded her head.

- That's one way of looking at it. The X and the Y of IT.
- So what am I to you, then? Some Slippery Serpent?
- I think you already know.
- Temptation?
- Excitement. Without excitement, creativity dies.

Skiddy was shaking his head.

-Three is a crowd. You are the she and he is the he.

Now, Rosa shook her head. He still seemed confused.

- Enlighten me, miss know-all!
- You are the Id of IT.
- So who is IT?
- We are. The X, the Y and Z of IT.
- X,Y,Z, QED.
- Quod Erat Demonstrandum

Johnny Gogan is a writer-director of films for cinema and tv, including the feature films The Last Bus Home (1997) which received the Best Film gong at the Cherbourg Festival of British and Irish Cinema and Mapmaker (2002), Special Jury Prize winner at Amiens International. His documentaries include Pobal Agus Plearaca (1999), The Adventures of Flannery (2007) and Na Coisithe (2009). Short films are Stephen (1990), winner of the Best Short Film award at Galway's Film Fleadh, The Bargain Shop (1993) and The Scaffolder Falls (2009). He was founding editor for Film Base of Film Ireland magazine in 1987 and more recently initiated Adaptation, a County Leitrim based festival which explores the relationship of Cinema and Literature. Ghost Writers is his first novel.

Ghost Writers

Dublin 1988:
The Poets of The Dublin Poetry Collective Prepare To Do Battle - With The Self

Johnny Gogan

For Tracy

Items should be returned on or before the last date shown below. Items not already requested by other borrowers may be renewed in person, in writing or by telephone. To renew, please quote the number on the barcode label. To renew online a PIN is required. This can be requested at your local library.
Renew online @ **www.dublincitypubliclibraries.ie**
Fines charged for overdue items will include postage incurred in recovery. Damage to or loss of items will be charged to the borrower.

Leabharlanna Poiblí Chathair Bhaile Átha Cliath
Dublin City Public Libraries

Date Due	Date Due	Date Due